ABOUT THIS BOOK

Welcome to the secluded mountain town of Havenwood Falls, home to sexy men, strong women, and neighbors who bite. Discover supernatural mystery, thrills, and romance in a place where everyone has a deep, dark, and often deadly secret.

Spirit Agent Tasha Young has never fit in. Her talents as a modern-day ghostbuster make her a loner by necessity. Her job is an easy one. Enter a haunted house, remove the misbehaving spirit, collect the cash, and move on to the next city. When she and her team are invited to Havenwood Falls for a special case, she quickly discovers that this retrieval isn't a simple bag and tag.

What lurks within is not one aura, but hundreds, and they all have their sights set on Tasha. With only five traps in her possession and a team member already sucked into the spirit world, Tasha is forced to come face to face with her greatest enemy: the Indrori.

If she can't find her way out of the spirit realm in time, the Indrori will win the prize he's been waiting centuries to claim. The future of Tasha, her team, and all of Havenwood Falls rests on the sultry black-haired beauty with the snake tattoo.

HAVENWOOD FALLS BOOKS

Forget You Not by Kristie Cook

Old Wounds by Susan Burdorf

Fate, Love & Loyalty by E.J. Fechenda

The Winged & the Wicked by T.V. Hahn & Kristie Cook

Alpha's Queen by Lila Felix

Ink & Fire by R.K. Ryals

Lose You Not by Kristie Cook

Tragic Ink by Heather Hildenbrand

Nowhere to Hide by Belinda Boring

Flames Among the Frost by Amy Hale

Rock Me Gently by Susan Burdorf

From the Embers by Amy Miles

Defying Gravity by Kallie Ross

Break Me Not by Kristie Cook

How the Dead Lie by Stacey Rourke

The Lurkers Within by Danielle Bannister

The Collector: Awakening by Kristie Cook, R.K. Ryals, Belinda Boring & Nadirah Foxx

Addicted to You by Belinda Boring

Affliction Mine by C.J. Pinard

The Ward & the Wanderers by T.V. Hahn

Toil & Trouble by Melissa Wright

Of Salt and Stars by Seven Jane

Redefined by Morgan Wylie

Betrayal Among the Frost by Amy Hale

Forever Loyal by E.J. Fechenda

Fate's Demand by Emily Cyr

The Wu & the Wand by T.V. Hahn

A Demon's Redemption by JD Nelson

Also try the YA line, Havenwood Falls High; the historical paranormal line, Legends of Havenwood Falls; the darker, sexier side of town, Havenwood Falls Sin & Silk; and the local supernatural college, Sun & Moon Academy.

Stay up to date at www.HavenwoodFalls.com

ALSO BY DANIELLE BANNISTER

Pulled: Book 1 in the Twin Flames Trilogy
Pulled Back: Book 2 in the Twin Flames Trilogy
Pulled Back Again: Book 3 in the Twin Flames Trilogy

Short Shorts
The ABC's of Dee
Enigma
Doppelganger
Must Love Coffee

Netherworld: Book 1 of The Hallowed Realms Trilogy with Amy Miles
Hollow Earth: Book 2 of The Hallowed Realms Trilogy with Amy Miles

THE LURKERS WITHIN

A HAVENWOOD FALLS NOVELLA

DANIELLE BANNISTER

This one goes out to my mom, Sharon Estes, who is my one and only alpha reader. She has to love me no matter what crap drafts I send her way. She reads them all—every single version—to help me find my "oopsies." Love you, Mom!

CHAPTER 1

"*W*ant me to take point?" Adam asked. His trap was raised high, like you might raise a gun going into a drug bust. His muscles flexed, showing delicious chocolate biceps. There were no two ways about it—that man was fine, but also not on my radar. Poor boy wanted some quaint Christian girl. That's definitely not me.

"No need," I said. "It's only a Class C spirit. It's not going anywhere."

Generally speaking, Class C spirits were harmless and confined to the places where they died, unless they were way older than this dipshit ghost, who chose to spend his afterlife tormenting a politician. We had him right where we wanted.

I was the last thing a pissed off ghost wanted to see, for good reason, too. I was the best spirit agent around. When a spirit felt me walk into a room, they knew their time was up. What can I say? I was infamous for being a bitch in both the human and spiritual realms. I wouldn't apologize for my skills. Or for being the best in my field. I was paid quite well by the feds for handling these "classified" cases. My job was simple: enter a haunted house, remove the misbehaving spirit, collect the cash, and move on to the next city. The world was none the wiser as to just how many ghosts they walked the earth with. Most were harmless. I only went after the ones that became a problem.

My team was called in this morning to remove a less-than-friendly Casper. This one was trapped in the attic. In a matter of minutes, the job would be over, and I could go back to the hotel, where I planned to sink into their hot tub. It really was the world's easiest job.

More often than not, I got assigned a Class B spirit. Those assholes became strong enough to emit sounds but were mostly harmless. Sure, I might end up with a scratch or two from the older ones, but those went away by the end of a day. Because they were so powerless, demonic spirits specialized in the psychological mind-game damage they could do to the humans they'd been forced to live with. This type of auras wrongly blamed humans for the reasons they were trapped between realms. These were the douchebags I specialized in. Grumpy spirits who liked to bite. That didn't scare me. I was into the rough stuff.

"Room is clear. Waiting on your call, Agent Young," the voice in my headpiece said. Ah, Winston was on today's mission. How wonderful. He was scared shitless of me. As he should have been.

"We go in when I say we go in, Winston."

Winston bumbled an apology, and I focused back on the door.

Beside me, Adam and my other team member, Eduardo, were all business, their traps poised and ready. They were so serious on these missions. For them, I imagined, this was pretty scary shit. Going up against a spirit wasn't as simple for them, mostly because they couldn't see them the way I could. The imagination was always worse than reality when it came to fear. I could see what I was after, so ghosts didn't frighten me in the least. The rest of the world was less fortunate.

To be clear, I couldn't see a ghost in the same way I could see a human. Spirits were not of this realm anymore, and therefore didn't hold the same shape as living, breathing humans. Instead, I saw the fragments of what was left of them—their auras. Their souls. It was sort of like looking at humans with heat-seeking glasses. A blob of pulsing energy. It wasn't crystal clear, but it was enough to be able to aim a trap accurately.

This baddie in the attic would be a cake walk. Normally, I wouldn't be called in for such an easy bag and tag but when this spirit took up residency at a VIP's place, my team was called in by the feds. Of course, if the FBI was asked about its Soul Searcher program and my place on it, it would deny any and all knowledge of me and the other spirit agents. Such was the risk of a confidential job. I was like a ghost myself. Now you see me, now you don't.

Only a few dozen teams like mine existed around the world, though most of them didn't have a team member like me. They had to rely on malfunctioning gadgets and incompetent tech to bring a spirit down. They didn't actually remove the spirit permanently. They simply pushed them somewhere else, but that wasn't my concern.

There were only five of us that the feds had in their employment who were also Recoverers. There were likely dozens more, but none of them wanted to be controlled by the bureaucracy. I didn't mind. It paid well. Being a Recoverer was another special skill of mine. I could bring back the recently crossed over. Well, I could bring them back if I could get to them within a few hours. I couldn't bring back anyone long dead like Elvis or Prince, though I totally would if I could.

Hell, a lot of those "near-death experiences" you read about? Nine times out of ten, it wasn't a miracle. It was a Recoverer sent to bring the soul back to the human realm. These souls weren't fully dead. They were stuck in the spirit realm and hadn't officially crossed over. Like purgatory, I guess. We snatched them out of the waiting rooms of death to live another day. I'd like to say why we brought back who we did had to do with noble reasons like true love, or they had the formula to cure cancer, or some shit like that, but it was usually because they owed money to the mob or were a family member of someone important. The feds charged a pretty penny for a recovery and only those with power could pay it.

I was recovering more souls than I trapped these days. It's like all the Recoverers decided to go on vacation at the same time. Lazy fuckers. No one had a strong work ethic anymore. But that was just fine by me. I'd happily take their fees.

Just then, Eduardo lifted his trap as he winked at me. Unlike

Adam, he got off on this part of the gig. He knew the men on this team were there only for show. I was the star, and he liked seeing me in action. Well, Eduardo liked seeing every aspect of me.

I don't say I was the star player merely because of my ability to see the spirits and bring back the dead, though those were pretty kick-ass skills. No, I was the leader of the team because I was the only one who could actually use the trap properly. I don't know if they were just slow on the trigger, aimed wrong, if their guns weren't calibrated right, or what. Whatever the reason, whatever the job, my traps were the only ones that took the spirits down. Adam and Eduardo were basically my backup dancers. I didn't need them at my side, but it sure made an intimidating picture to the spirit.

Nodding, I gave Adam the signal to kick down the attic door. Did we need to break the door to get to the spirit? Hell no. Breaking shit was for the politician's benefit. Might as well make him believe it was harder than it looked, right? Smoke and mirrors. That's all ghost hunting and politics were, after all.

Adam went in first, followed by Eduardo. Each of them shouted for the ghost to show itself. This was really quite a ridiculous thing to say to a ghost, especially with me on the job, but it made them feel useful and masculine to yell.

The ghost was there, plain as day to me. Eduardo and Adam watched my face to follow where I was looking, so they would know where to aim their traps. Usually, I had to walk around to find the thing cowering in a corner, but this spirit was hovering right in front of me. Almost as if it wanted to be found. In fact, I swear it cocked its head when it saw me.

"Why, hello," I said with a smirk.

Adam and Eduardo raised their traps to where I was focused, but my trap remained at my side as I studied the boldness of the spirit. This was unusual behavior for a spirit. They were typically more skittish when they knew their time was up. Color me intrigued.

"Fire?" Adam whispered when I stalled the command.

"Not yet. I need to check on one thing first," I said, tapping against my earpiece. My eyes never left the aura. Though I couldn't see actual eyes, I had the sneaking suspicion its focus was directly on me as well.

"Go ahead, Agent Young," Winston said in my earpiece.

"Is my room ready at the Ritz?"

"Yes. I have booked a king bed, just like you asked."

"Good," I purred. "Eduardo and I plan on making good use of it later." There was a silence on the other end of the com, which assured me I had made poor Winston blush. I knew full well all our conversations during missions were recorded. I didn't say such things to torment Winston, but to annoy my commanding officer, Agent Duncan. He didn't care for the fact that Eduardo and I were screwing around. It was jealousy, pure and simple. They all got that way when I tired of them.

"I suppose it's time to trap this spirit and go play, eh, Eduardo?" I whispered into his ear.

His lips curled into a mischievous smile for a half a second, but then he refocused on the mission, like a good boy.

I lifted my trap in one fluid movement, waiting for the spirit to make a run for it, but it didn't move. It held its ground in front of me. Smart spirit. It would have been wasted energy trying to escape from me.

"Your time is coming," the female-sounding spirit said, though only I could hear it. I raised my eyebrows, impressed in spite of myself. They normally couldn't communicate. It took too much energy. Those four words likely drained her completely. She was easy prey now. Not that she wasn't before.

"Yeah, yeah, we all meet our maker soon enough. Right now, though, it's your turn," I said, before walking right up to her. I pointed the gun to where her head was and pulled the trigger. My wrist singed a bit from the kickback of the gun, but it was a small price to pay.

"Target acquired."

I handed the trap to Adam, who held onto it like it was worth more than gold. Spirits fascinated him. He longed to be able to see them as I did. He always took meticulous notes after each capture, begging me to describe each spirit in as much detail as possible.

Apparently, saying it looked like colored smoke wasn't enough for him. I wished he could see an aura, just once, so he'd get off my back about them.

Eduardo was less professional about the completion of our mission and opted to grab my ass instead. He pulled me close for a congratulatory kiss. I wasn't about to object. That man knew how to use his tongue.

"Get a room," Adam groaned. Eduardo and I did this sort of thing all the time, so you'd think he'd be used to it by now, but his prudish ways always left me feeling a little dirty. In the good way.

"Great idea," I said. I'd had enough work for one day. It was well past time to let off some steam. Eduardo was the perfect way to do it, too. We left the attic, arm in arm, leaving all thoughts of the job behind.

CHAPTER 2

Three months and nine captured spirits later, I still wasn't tired of Eduardo, which was a record for me. I don't know if it was because he was Latino and knew how to treat a woman, or if I might have been falling for him. It had to be the first option. I didn't fall for anyone. I left them too soon to allow for that. Eduardo made me break my own rule of no more than two dates. Working with a guy you were also sleeping with, however, complicated that rule. It wasn't as though I could just disappear from his life, like I did with every other guy. It was easy to ditch guys I met when we traveled. Our team was never in one spot for more than a few days. Eduardo was a harder man to shake because he was paid to follow me.

This thing with him was getting out of hand, though. I had to cut this off. I couldn't be the monogamous partner he wanted. That just wasn't me. I was too much of a flirt. After our Thanksgiving break, I'd call it off. It wasn't fair to him. I'd spend the week screwing his brains out, then I'd toss him to the curb. It was a solid plan.

That's when I felt his hands press warmly against my breasts. The way he breathed hot against my neck alerted me to the fact that our morning coffee was about to be postponed.

"You're up early," I teased, reaching my hand around to help him achieve his full potential.

"I say we skip the gym and do our morning workout in bed," he murmured.

"You riding me sounds so much better than me riding the elliptical," I said in my husky voice that drove him wild.

For the next half hour or so, we "worked out" so hard it would have made even Jane Fonda proud. When we had finished, he rolled off me, slapping me on the ass as he did. He was still frisky. Good.

"Hey, Tasha, how many scales do you have filled in now?" Eduardo asked, running his hand along my back, which displayed an outlined tattoo of a Mexican King serpent. It really was an impressive piece of work. My torso held much of the snake's body as it wrapped twice around me. The tail ended at my hairline on the back of my neck while the black head of it disappeared into my 'Garden of Eden.' The individual scales, numbering over a hundred, were outlined and waiting to be fully inked in. A full-body tat like this would likely take twenty or more years to fill in. In its outline form, however, it still made for an epic piece.

"How many? Um . . . a lot." I laughed as I watched his eyes rake over my naked body. I'd lost count of how many were completed, since I started with the ones on my back first. I hated needles and really didn't want to watch it being done, so being face down for as much of the process as possible was ideal. For someone not keen on needles, perhaps a full-body tattoo was stupid, but the idea of it came to me in a dream one night. The fact that I had a birthmark that looked a bit scale-like cemented the design for me. I hated those ugly birthmarks, and they seemed to keep cropping up more often as I aged. This design disguised them perfectly. Even the tattoo artist thought it was pretty badass. Hurt like a motherfucker though.

I craned my neck in an effort to see the scales he was staring at, but it was useless. I wasn't as bendable as I was in my twenties. "I'm guessing there's probably like twenty-five by now?"

Eduardo shook his head. "That looks like a lot more than twenty-five. I'll have to count them one day," he said, leaning over to lick one, "with my tongue."

"You always were a stickler for actual data," I replied.

He slid off the bed then and tossed a sheet on me, so I wouldn't get cold. He was thoughtful, that one. "I'm gonna hit the shower."

"Mmm," I said, hugging the sheet around me. His cologne was intoxicating all on its own. Still, not a reason to keep a guy around. After this break, I'd need to be reassigned to a new team. Again. Maybe I'd try the London office. Lots more pasty-looking guys with bad teeth there. Less temptation.

"Hey, Tasha, get your ass in here with me!" Eduardo yelled over the noise of the rushing water.

"I'll be there in a minute." I grinned. No harm in enjoying him while I could. Though I needed to check in with work. I still hadn't gotten the official "you're clear for vacation" message, even though I put in for the time months ago. Sure, the work was easy, but the constant travel was weighing on me. I was looking forward to parking it in one place for the week.

Yanking the sheet off me, I yawned and walked, buck-naked, over to my phone. It was tucked into the back pocket of my pants.

As soon as I turned it on, notifications started pouring in, which was unusual. I didn't have friends or family—at least, none that knew this number—so I knew something big at work must have gone down overnight. Especially when all fifteen messages said the same thing.

AGENT YOUNG, CALL THIS NUMBER ASAP.

"So much for being off next week. Asshats." Blowing out a breath, I glanced at the number. It wasn't my normal FBI contact, but that happened now and again. An undercover op would need help, so they called my team in. The feds were the only ones with my number, so it had to be legit.

Tossing the phone on the bed, I went to join Eduardo. Whoever it was, they could wait ten more minutes. Maybe twenty.

Forty minutes later, thank you very much, I sent Eduardo down to the lobby for coffee. I hated the crap they pawned off in the room. Tasted like caffeinated cardboard. I missed my own four-cup coffee pot, ironically. I couldn't remember the last time I slept in my apartment back in Soho. Was it weeks now, or months? Ultimately, it didn't matter since the feds picked up the bill, but there was something about having a space of your own. A space you could claim. With each passing year, I found myself longing more and more for that elusive word—home.

Sighing, I punched the number given me into my cell and plopped on the unmade bed. The smell of our morning adventure still lingered on the sheets as I lay down, waiting to find out where I was being shipped off to next. This, by far, was the worst part of the job. Always leaving.

CHAPTER 3

"*H*avenwood Falls?" I asked, pulling out my laptop to search for its location as my contact prattled on. "Where the hell is that?"

"It's a small town in Colorado. Don't bother looking it up. It's not on any map. Remote town with lots of mountains. Pack layers. November may be warm in Jacksonville, Agent Young, but it won't be in Havenwood Falls."

I closed my laptop. "How did you know where I am?"

"I just know, Agent Young. Can we skip the fifty questions?"

Well then, Captain Dickhead wasn't a chatter. Great. I worked with men like this all the time. Alpha types who felt they needed to talk down to the female of the species. Damn it all if I didn't usually find men like that sexy.

As Dicky spoke, I did a mental inventory of the few clothes I had: Two pairs of black pants, three white button-up dress shirts, two black bras (because why wear a white bra when a black one through a white shirt could be so titillating), three pairs of shoes—two of them heels— and one black leather jacket. I'd likely need to grab something warmer when I got to the airport; something easily left behind on the plane ride back when I left. I traveled light. Lived light. Everything I owned fit in one travel suitcase. Necessities only. That's the reality I knew.

"Agent Young, your flight leaves in four hours. There will be someone waiting to pick you up from the airport. I trust that will be enough time to get your team ready?"

I pulled my thoughts out of my carryon and back into the conversation.

"Yes. Absolutely."

"The tickets are being left with the front desk of your hotel. Your fee has already been wired to your account. Any questions?" he asked. Now that the details were sorted, he sounded bored.

"Yeah. Just one. Who are you?"

Agent Duncan usually called my assignments in. Not that I minded not hearing from Duncan. He was a snore-fest. This guy, while arrogant as fuck, at least sounded sexy as all get out. Hell, this guy might be just the thing to get my mind off Eduardo.

"I'm the guy paying you to do your job, Agent Young."

Well, well, well. I was annoying him. Good. Men like him needed playing with.

"I meant, what is your name?" I asked, matching his arrogant tone.

"You'd better start packing, Agent. Let your team know we're counting on their A game for this capture."

Great. This was going to be one of those top-secret missions the feds sent me on where everything was need-to-know, including who was in charge.

"It's the only way I play," I said.

"So I've heard." With that, there was a click and the call was ended.

Eduardo came in just then with our coffees and two bagels perched precariously on top. I relieved him of one set.

"Eat fast. We've got a mission. Flight leaves in four hours."

"I thought you were off next week?"

My phone vibrated then, alerting me of an incoming wire. I showed him the screen. He gave a low whistle. I nodded. "For this fee, I'm available."

Eduardo nodded. "I'll call Adam."

Adam was staying on the floor above us. He learned the hard way to never be below our room. Eduardo and I were too noisy. Adam was always ready to leave at a moment's notice, so I had no doubt he'd be here within five minutes, which was a good thing. Four hours wasn't a lot of prep time, but our cover stories always remained the same: Adam played my husband, and Eduardo, because of his baby face, played our bi-racial son. *Leave It to Beaver* had nothing on our motley crew.

Playing Adam's wife was easy, because Adam was a fine piece of man. Standing at six foot one, he had dark cocoa skin and bicep muscles for days. He was uber religious, though, so he had no interest in me and my "whorish" ways. He harped on me a lot about all the men I slept around with, but I knew he secretly wished I'd find someone and finally settle down. He had a good heart, that one. He was going to make some virginal woman very happy one day. It just sure as hell wouldn't be me.

At each new assignment, we adopted our roles and played house for a few days until the spirits got close enough to trap them. Older spirits could move around more than the chick we bagged in the attic a few months ago. As awesome as I was at trapping spirits, I couldn't walk through walls. Playing chase with a ghost was not my idea of a good time. Hence the cover. If we went into a house with Class B spirits with traps blazing, we'd never get as close as I needed to be to bag them. I had to literally be right on top of them in order for the trap to work. Sneak attacks were the only way to land these assholes without all the Tom & Jerry–style chasing.

"Where are we headed?" Eduardo asked after he hung up with Adam.

"Havenwood Falls. Ever heard of it?" I asked.

He shook his head, making his lush curls bounce as he did. "Should I?"

I shrugged. "No. I guess it's somewhere in West Bumfuck, Colorado."

"Great. Adam and I will blend right in." He smirked, showing off not only his cute-as-fuck dimples, but his golden Puerto Rican skin.

"That town will be crazy jealous of the white chick with two colored studs on her arms."

He grabbed me by the waist and pulled me to him.

"I'd do her," he said.

I laughed. "You have. Twice just this morning. Unfortunately, we don't have time for round three. We have to get to the airport."

"Party pooper," he said playfully, but promptly went to pack his things. I watched his backside as he walked to the dresser. *I think we'll need to squeeze in a mile-high-club visit.*

CHAPTER 4

*W*hen my team was picked up at the airport in a cheesy-looking tourist bus that would have put the Mystery Machine to shame, I couldn't help but think that bus was going to be the weirdest thing I'd see all day. I was so, so wrong.

After a four-hour drive, the little bus that could managed to haul our asses up the windy, snow-covered, and fog-ridden mountainside. We were driven into a town that looked like a replica of Mayberry. Not even joking. For starters, the center of Havenwood Falls looked more like a movie set than a real place. It just looked too perfect. Magical, somehow.

In the middle of town was a squared off section that held a park area with a fountain dead center and a gazebo off to the right of it. Like a proper, old fashioned gazebo. What town still had those? It wasn't even Thanksgiving yet, and there were Christmas decorations everywhere. No respect for Thanksgiving. I wanted to hurl. Towns like this were so not ready for the likes of me and my crew. I dug out my cell to check the time, and only then did I realize what day it was— Black Friday. That's why there were so many people out and about. I missed Thanksgiving completely while traveling here to this bullshit assignment. How pathetic was I that I forgot a major holiday like that?

It was just one of the many ways my job consumed every aspect of my life.

"Hey, we missed Thanksgiving," I said to Eduardo.

He shrugged. "I don't really like turkey anyway. Besides, this place makes up for it. Check out those slopes!" His eyes were still focused outside the window on the mountain beyond. I was about to scold Adam for not reminding me, but then I remembered he was Canadian.

Surrounding the square was an odd assortment of businesses. Your typical things like coffee shops, town offices, and hair stylist and such, but they all had hippy-dippy names like Into the Mystic and Shear Magic. I knew cannabis was legal in Colorado, but these store names were out there even for a pothead.

That's when we passed by the Haven Saloon.

"Praise Jesus. We're saved. They have a bar," I said, to no one in particular. Eduardo and Adam were too busy looking at this bizarre little town with far more wonder than I was. I wasn't sure what it was, but something about this town felt very, very wrong, while at the same time, a little bit right.

"There's a ski shop! Tasha, we *have* to go skiing," Eduardo beamed.

"Um, we're only here for a week. I don't know how much skiing time there will be." I looked up at the mountains, though, and was surprised to see whitecaps when there were only a few inches on the ground. "Have you ever been skiing?" I asked Eduardo, raising my eyebrow.

"No! Which is why we should try it!"

Adam and I exchanged a glance. Eduardo, though he was great in the sack, was not known for his athletic prowess outside of the bedroom.

"Let's just focus on the assignment first, shall we?" Adam said, taking the pressure off me to tell him no.

"Fine, but then we are so all going!" he said, bouncing up and down in his seat like the teenager he was about to portray. It made me laugh despite the surroundings of this bizarre little town.

The small group on the bus filed out one by one. Adam and

Eduardo grabbed our gear while I looked around for where the hell we were supposed to go to now. Dicky hadn't exactly been clear, and he wasn't returning my texts.

"Agent Young?"

I spun around and saw a man dressed in black holding a sign with my name on it.

"That's us," I said.

"Right this way." He gestured to his black car with tinted glass that screamed FBI. Way to be inconspicuous and likely blow our cover, jackass.

"Damn, girl. We're being treated like royalty," Eduardo sang as he hopped into the car. "Who is this dude, anyway?"

"No clue. Someone who clearly doesn't understand the concept of working undercover."

Adam and I exchanged a glance. He felt it too. There was something unusual about this mission. We never got wined and dined this much. Something was fishy.

As our driver took us out of the center of the town, we realized he wasn't going to speak to us. Every question we asked went unanswered, which meant he must have been given specific orders to keep quiet. Fine by me. The sooner we got there, the sooner I could find out the assignment, finish the job, then get the hell out of dodge. This place was making my skin itch. It was too perfect, which meant it was hiding a secret. It didn't help that all the tourists and hippies were gawking at us, I just knew it. Didn't matter where I went. People always stared at me. Yes, I am a freak. Move on with your lives, people!

We made a left on Thirteenth Street, which seemed fitting considering the supernatural twist to our jobs. We stayed on that road until the car pulled up beside a light sage-colored house. It didn't look like a haunted house you might imagine in a book or movie, but houses with the most demonic spirits didn't. They looked like normal, cute little houses.

Just like this one. The hairs on my arm went up. This was bad. Very bad. Whatever was in that house wasn't something we'd been up against before.

Once I got outside of the car, my suspicions were confirmed. In that moment, I knew *exactly* why our team had been called in. My stomach lurched. This was no Class B spirit.

"Tasha? You okay?"

Adam had a bag in his hand, while Eduardo was pulling out the rest from the trunk. The driver stayed in the car, the engine still running. He must have known what we were up against, because he had no plans to stick around.

"Everything's hunky-dory, babe," I said, making direct eye contact with Adam to make sure he understood. "Just got a little carsick is all."

Hunky-dory was a code word. It warned the team that all was not, well, hunky-dory. It told them that I'd felt the presence of intense dark energy. There was something predominantly evil oozing out of that house. If my senses were right, and they always were, there was far more than one baddie inside, to boot.

"You have the key, *Mom?*" Eduardo asked, slipping into character and letting me know he got the message. Normally, we didn't have to put on our act until we got inside, because ghosts couldn't see that far, but this was old energy, possibly the oldest I'd ever come up against. The older the spirit, the farther they could see.

I took the small carryon Adam had, which held one of our five traps. They were hidden among our belongings for ease of access. They had to be close by, but also hidden, lest we spook what we were hunting. I had a sinking feeling that what we were packing wasn't going to be enough. Whatever spirits were lurking within were a patient group. They were gathering for something. Something big.

My muscles tensed in anticipation as I put on a plastic smile. We were being watched. Better make it convincing. Since our contact wasn't providing me with the information I needed to formulate a plan, I would have to figure it out myself, which meant seeing exactly what we were up against with my own eyes before I called headquarters and reamed someone's ass out for sending us in here so unprepared.

"Let's go see our new home for the week," I said, sounding way more chipper than I felt.

CHAPTER 5

From all outward appearances, the inside of the house looked like any other you might find listed in an Airbnb ad. The appliances were new and all stainless steel. All the surfaces had been dusted. The path to the house had been shoveled and sanded. The sun beamed inside through large bay windows, doing its best to remove the shadow that hung over the place like a living, breathing beast.

Everything inside looked like it had been handpicked by an interior designer, save for a creepy-ass wooden doll perched on the mantle. She had on a green dress from what looked like the 1700s. The paint had chipped on the nose and neck, making her look like she'd been smudged with dirt. The dress she wore had yellowed from the sun. She had an apron and bonnet over the dress. A servant. Not the sort of doll you'd usually see kept over the years. It was the eyes that made her creepy, though. No color to them. Just black orbs that seemed to follow me as I walked. I had to turn it around. It gave me the heebie-jeebies, and I didn't scare easy.

Eduardo gave me a weird look when I turned around from the doll. I tried to communicate with just my eyes to use extreme caution in this house, but Adam and Eduardo were already on the defensive. While still trying to keep up the cover of a happy-go-lucky family on a ski vacation, they clutched their bags tightly, ready to take out their traps the moment I gave the order.

"Cool digs," Eduardo said in his best teenybopper voice. "I'm going to go check out the bedrooms."

"I'll go with you," Adam said. "No way are you claiming the biggest room, kid."

I nodded, understanding they were really doing some surveillance. Not that it would help. Eduardo and Adam wouldn't be able to see anything out of the ordinary. Not like I did. Sometimes they could feel a temperature shift, though, if a spirit was old enough. My guess was they'd be covered in gooseflesh by the time they came back, if the upstairs was anything like the downstairs view.

My mouth fought to stay closed and conceal my true horror while I looked at what appeared to be an empty living room to human eyes. In reality, I was in a living room that was filled with no less than six spirits, each one circling around me. They weren't attacking or trying to latch on to me. They seemed to be patiently observing. I had no doubt there would be more in the bedrooms.

Poltergeist was my first thought. We must have been on an ancient burial ground, or some shit like that. Why else would there be so many spirits in one spot? Then another thought struck me. Had there been a mass murder here? That was a high possibility, too. My contact hadn't mentioned anything about what we were up against, but I was racking my brain for logical reasons so many spirits would be in the same house. Spirits weren't as mobile as movies made them out to be. They couldn't just travel around from house to house. They were tied to the space where they died. So what the hell happened here?

I thought back, trying to remember all the case files I'd read from other spirit agents about mass spirit gatherings, while I placed my bag on the floor. The only one that came even close was one from Sweden about ten years ago, when a spirit agent discovered four souls in the same house who had somehow merged themselves into one spirit. The case was dismissed by other spirit agents as unsolved. Other than that, I couldn't think of any other case file that had this many spirits in one place.

Keeping up my disguise, I plopped down on the couch and scanned the room, appearing to appreciate the view from the bay window, but I was instead assessing the color of the auras in the room.

Spirits gave off different colors based on their mood. Yellow meant they were at peace and content. Those were, by far, the easiest ones to capture. The blue auras were confused spirits. They didn't understand why they were in between worlds and often didn't believe they were dead in the first place.

A confused spirit was what most people came across. They caused minimal damage in that they mostly only scared the shit out of their owners with their moaning and floor creaking. They were more annoying than harmful, but even spirit pests needed an exterminator.

Red auras were the worst. They were the pissed off baddies. The most demonic ones. They hated the human realm and the fact they were stuck in it. They would hurt anyone they could. It took massive amounts of energy and years as a spirit to be able to leave any sort of physical mark on a human, but it still fucking hurt. That said, red auras were rare. In my years as a spirit agent, I'd only come across a handful of them. This room alone held six of them.

How the hell was I supposed to trap this many demonic spirits with only five traps? We couldn't. We literally couldn't. In fact, it was extremely dangerous for any of us to be here. I had to get my team out, now.

"Hey, Mom?" Eduardo asked suddenly from upstairs. There was a thread of panic in his voice. Adrenaline rushed through me as I wondered if I was too late.

I ran up the stairs to find Eduardo standing over Adam's limp body. Adam was sprawled out on one of the beds, his eyes closed. There was no blood, no sign of foul play; it simply looked as though Adam had decided to take a nap, which we both knew was not what was happening.

"What's wrong, peanut?" I asked, highly aware we were being watched. I didn't want to spook them into doing anything else rash. I rubbed Eduardo's shoulder hard, trying to hide my panic.

"Um . . . I think Dad passed out," he said, clearly as freaked out as

I was but trying hard to maintain the cover. "I went to check out the other room, and when I came back, he was like that."

My blood began to race as I walked over to Adam. I pressed my hand against his forehead, like a wife would do for a potentially sick husband, and watched closely for signs of life.

"Oh, honey, Daddy's fine," I said in a whisper. He was still breathing, but his skin was colder than it should have been. *Shit.* "I think he's just exhausted from the trip. Jet lag is a real thing. It can knock you right out." I took one last look at Adam then turned my attention back to Eduardo. "Why don't you and I go for a walk, check out the town while your dad sleeps? There looked like some great lunch options to try out."

Eduardo was tense, but he nodded, looking back one last time at Adam. I knew he wasn't okay with leaving Adam in this condition, but he would listen to my orders. I'd fill him in as soon as we got clear of the house.

"Yeah, okay. We should come back later. Let him rest."

"Good idea, kid," I said tousling his hair.

I looped my arm through his and led him as casually down the stairs as I humanly could. We needed to get out of this house stat and contact headquarters. Someone needed to tell us what the hell was going on here.

For a half a second, I thought we weren't going to be able to leave as I noticed all the red auras following us to the exit, but when I put my hand on the knob, it opened, bringing with it the freedom of the cool afternoon air.

When we had walked several blocks, to be far enough that I couldn't feel the spirits watching us anymore, I dug out my cell phone. Agent Duncan was going to get an earful from me. I wanted to know who the hell called me and why. I didn't trust my contact as far as I could throw him. When I tried the line, however, the call never went through.

"Damn it!" I held up the phone and tried again. Still nothing.

"What just happened back there?" Eduardo asked, rushing to keep up with my stride. While he couldn't see what I had, I was sure he knew that whatever went down wasn't good.

"They took Adam, that's what's happened," I shouted. I was pissed.

Eduardo stopped walking. None of our team had ever been taken into the spirit world. In fact, it had only ever happened once in my time as a spirit agent. Only a Recoverer, like myself, could bring back a taken soul, but only within twelve hours of the attack. After that, they were stuck in purgatory while their body lay in a coma. Brain dead, doctors called it. More like soul-sucked.

"Someone has some serious explaining to do," I said as I tried my contact's number instead. At first, I didn't think it was going to go through, then the line finally connected.

"Agent Young. I didn't expect to hear from you so soon. Done already, are you?" my contact said on the end of the line. He seemed amused. I was about to wipe that smile off his smug face.

"Cut the shit. I need to know what the fuck my team is up against."

There was a silence and some shuffling noises, like he was trying to find a private place to have this conversation.

"What happened?" he whispered.

"They've taken one of my agents, that's what's happened! There are at least a dozen demonic spirits in that house. Now we're up against a clock to get Adam's soul back, which means I have to drag my ass back in there, so I need you to tell me what the hell is going on!" I yelled, garnering some stares from the joggers on the other side of the road. Fuck them. I couldn't care less about my cover right now. Adam's life was hanging in the balance.

"Meet me in town square. There's a coffee shop called Coffee Haven. I'll explain what I can."

It was my turn to stop walking.

"Wait. You're *here?* In Havenwood Falls?" We didn't have any spirit agent FBI branches in Colorado. Who the hell was this guy?

"Ten minutes, Agent Young."

The call ended, and I stared at my cell for a moment.

"Something is seriously messed up here," I said to Eduardo as he approached me.

"Ya think? Why didn't you recover Adam back there? You said he was taken. Why didn't you just pull him back into this plane? Why did you make us leave? What aren't you telling me, Tasha?'

"There wasn't time to recover him. Not without one, or both of us, being taken next. We're not up against one spirit, Eduardo. It's a fucking legion."

Eduardo stopped walking as he let that sink in. He'd never taken down a legion before. None of us had. It wasn't what we were trained for, so our contact had better have a damn good plan and explanation for all of this, because I was officially out of ideas.

CHAPTER 6

*W*e didn't need ten minutes to reach the center of town. I would have been there faster if Eduardo hadn't been slowing me down by asking me a million questions I didn't have the answers to. No, I didn't know how they took Adam. No, I didn't know why there were so many in the house. No, I wasn't sure how we were going to save Adam. All of my answers started with "No." I had no fucking clue what was going on. Add to that the fact that walking in heels, in the winter, with just my thin leather jacket meant not only was I pissed at being lied to, I was also cold. I was in a foul mood. I almost felt bad for our contact. The hellstorm he was about to endure wouldn't be pretty.

"I hate snow," Eduardo said beside me, trying to stomp out the snow from the treads of his sneakers once we made it to the center of town. Eduardo hated any temperature below eighty degrees, so this place wasn't rubbing off well on either of us.

"Says the guy who wanted to ski earlier." I snorted.

"Skiing and walking around in sneakers in four inches of snow are two very different things, chica."

"Yeah, well nothing about this mission is making me warm and fuzzy either," I said, pulling my jacket around me tighter.

Our meeting spot was easy enough to find once we made it to the center of town. The smell of caffeine permeated onto the sidewalk. Coffee Haven was on Main Street, wedged in between a massive book store called Shelf Indulgence and a consignment store of some kind. Two types of stores I never frequented. I hadn't read a book since high school, and I never bought anything used.

Eduardo was still peppering me with questions as I yanked open the door of the coffee shop harder than I needed to. The small bell above the door chimed, making me roll my eyes. Of course there was a damn bell on the door. This town was too perfect. I didn't trust it. My eyes darted around the room, looking for my contact, or someone who looked like they might be, but found that it was deserted, save for an older couple in the corner sipping their drinks. I glanced at my phone to check the time. We were early.

"Should we get a coffee?" Eduardo asked. Finally, a question of his I could answer.

"I'd rather have a shot of whiskey, but I suppose caffeine will have to do."

He nodded. We were both caffeine addicts, and with Adam taken, I knew this was going to be one long-ass day, so I'd need to keep my eyes and brain alert, which meant strong coffee. And lots of it. The air here was messing me up and giving me a wicked headache. The caffeine would need to do double duty today.

"I'll get it." I gestured toward a table near the window for him to sit at. I shrugged out of my coat and handed it to Eduardo, who took it and moved to the table I indicated without saying anything else. *Good boy.*

As I walked up to order, I was taken aback by the massive marble counter. I highly doubted it was the real thing, given the size and the budget a shop like this might have, but nevertheless, it was still impressive for a joint like this.

I checked out the rest of the shop while I waited for the barista, who had his back turned while he was on the phone. The ambiance here was bizarre. There were plants everywhere, as well as artwork, and random crystals placed in every nook and cranny. It was a hippy-lover's dream.

While I waited, I placed my elbows down, being sure to squeeze my breasts together to give the guy working the counter the best view. I had a nice rack. Seemed a pity not to show it off whenever I could. Plus, I loved how it messed with guys' brains. Flirting was something that came naturally to me. Even in times of high stress like this. It was a coping mechanism to be sure, but what a fun one to have.

The barista finally hung up and then turned around. When he saw me, his eyes became unavoidably glued to the show I was offering. I smirked. He cleared his throat as he approached me and pushed up his dark rimmed glasses. I couldn't help but notice him play with his wedding band. Guilty conscience much?

"What can I get ya?" he asked. His voice shook a little, letting me know how nervous I made him. Good.

"How about a name, for starters?"

"Um, I'm. Um. Davis. My name is Davis. I'm the manager here. How can I help you?"

I loved his obvious discomfort.

"What's good here, Davis?" I batted my eyes for good measure, 'cause why not?

"We make a mean latte."

"I'm sure you do." I licked my lips nice and slow. "Two coffees. Black. I like my drinks dark and strong. Just like my men."

His eyes widened again, but he quickly came back to reality.

"Right away," he said, turning to grab two mugs, seemingly grateful to get away from me.

I turned around and leaned my back on the counter, waiting for our drinks. Eduardo had his cell out, probably trying to get a signal. It didn't seem to work outside of local calls, since my contact was the only one I had been able to reach. It made absolutely no sense. Or, more likely, something was seriously messed up about this town. There had to be a reason I couldn't contact the outside world, and I was betting it had nothing to do with faulty cell towers.

"Here ya go," Davis said from behind me.

I turned back around and noticed the start of a tattooed compass on his hand. The bulk of it disappeared up the sleeve of his shirt. How cute. He was a tat-tease.

"Nice ink," I said, ready to do a little toying of my own.

He glanced down at his hand. "Thanks. I got it at Tragic Ink right there on Eighth Street, if you're interested in getting one yourself." He pointed out the window to a building on the square, but I didn't turn to look.

"Oh, I think I've got enough ink, don't you?" I asked, lifting the bottom of my shirt to expose the massive snake coils wrapped around my waist. Davis's eyes nearly fell out of his head. "I'd show you where the head is, but I'd get arrested for indecent exposure."

I bit my bottom lip. Playing with men was just too much fun.

"Thanks for the coffee," Eduardo said, suddenly at my side. He pulled my shirt down for me.

"Oh, are you jealous?" I snickered as we walked back to the table.

"I'm not the jealous type, but overt flirting like that is going to get you in trouble one of these days," he said.

"I'm counting on it."

As soon as we sat down, our contact walked in. It had to be him; otherwise, I would be very disappointed. Mr. Tall, Dark, and Handsome himself walked into the shop, sticking out like a sore thumb against the granola decor. There was no way he was FBI. People that good-looking didn't work for the feds.

I tried not to drool as I took him in. He wore a dark gray overcoat, which he removed and slid over his arm with a practiced ease. The dark silk suit and crisp white undershirt he wore, paired with gorgeous stubble across his jaw and no wedding ring, had me drooling. *Lickable. So very lickable.* Maybe this mission wasn't such a bust after all.

"Special Agent Young. Agent Lopez." He nodded to each of us as he sat down across from us without revealing his own name.

"Davis," he said, not taking his eyes off me, "I need a witch's brew."

"Sure thing, Mr. Bishop."

I clasped my hands and put them on the table.

"Bishop? So that's your name. Funny. I'm not familiar with any

Bishops in the Bureau," Eduardo snapped. He was jealous. They needn't fight over me. I'd gladly share.

That observation garnered a glare to my partner.

"Tell your lapdog to go fetch something outside. Then we'll talk," Bishop said, turning his deep blue eyes back on me. *Damn.* He was sexy.

"Whatever you need to say to Tasha, you can say to me," Eduardo said, putting his arm around me, effectively marking his territory.

Agent Bishop leaned back in his chair and looked at me, clearly indicating this conversation was going nowhere until Eduardo left. He knew he held all the cards. I had no choice. I had to play his game. For now. Adam couldn't wait for this pissing match to play out.

"Why don't you go take a walk?" I asked, turning to Eduardo, trying to placate him with my eyes. I'd make this up to him when this nightmare was over.

His displeasure was written all over his face.

"Oh, is that how it is, is it?" His tone spoke volumes about how pissed he was at me, but there was little I could do, given our current situation.

"I don't have time to play games with this guy, Eduardo. Adam needs our help, and this dipshit may hold the key." That seemed to soften the blow a bit, because he nodded once.

"Fine." He stood up fast, grabbing his coat and coffee. "I'll be right outside." Eduardo and Bishop had a mini staring contest, but Eduardo eventually backed down and huffed his way outside.

"Threatened by a little boy, are we, Mr. Bishop?"

He leaned across the table. "I don't share. Anything."

I matched his inward lean with one of my own, being sure to showcase the girls.

"Well, you've got it. Now, would you mind telling me what the fuck is going on in that house, or do I have to whip it out of you, Mr. Bishop?"

His eyes seemed slightly amused. "You couldn't get me to do anything I didn't want to, even if you were down on your knees, Agent Young."

Oh, he was good. Playing hard to get too. I smirked. "Call me Tasha."

I extended a hand, but he didn't take it, as though proving his point. Maybe he didn't want to play with me. That would be a first for me.

"Roman," he said when I took my hand away. "Well, Tasha, as you've probably deduced, I am not with the FBI."

"No shit. Everything about this mission hasn't smelled right, starting with you. Now why don't you tell me why you brought me here?"

Davis arrived just then with Roman's drink. It looked like a regular black coffee, but there was a definite shimmer to it. Like there was oil in it or something. Probably coconut oil or some healthy shit.

"What the hell is that?"

"It's mine and, therefore, not your concern."

"You know what?" I said as calmly as I could. "You're absolutely right. I don't care about you, or the sewage you're about to drink. I only care about my partner, Adam. Who took him, and why did you bring us here?"

He smiled. "That's more like it." Roman picked up his cup and took a slow and careful sip before he answered my question. "I invited you here because I've heard you're the best in the business."

My eyes narrowed, and I licked my lips. "I'm the best at *everything* I do."

He smiled as though that was exactly the answer he was expecting. "I'm counting on that." He took another sip as though we weren't under the gun for recovering Adam's soul. "Ms. Youn—Tasha, have you ever heard of the Indrori?"

"That another one of your fancy coffee drinks?"

He closed his eyes for a moment, as though he were trying not to scold me for being insolent.

"No. An Indrori is an agglomeration of spirits. One demonic ghost who has figured out a way to absorb the spirits of other ghosts around them, giving it strength unlike anything the world has ever seen."

"Well, that's where you're wrong. The world has seen it. Well, a select few have. My agency knows all about these soul clusters," I hedged, trying to remember more information on that one case file I was thinking about earlier.

He pushed his cup aside. "I'm sure your 'agency' has seen a few feeble couplings peppered here and there. I, however, am referring to something far more aggressive."

I'd play along, if only to get a clearer picture about what I was up against. "Go on."

"We believe that this Indrori has a hundred souls or more currently within his control. He appears to be able to merge and unmerge with these souls at will, according to our source."

I blinked at him, fighting the urge to roll my eyes. The guy was clearly yanking my chain.

"A hundred-plus souls . . . all under the control of one aura? That's not possible. You should have stopped at ten. I might have believed you then." There was no way. No way was a thing like that possible if I didn't know about it. "I would have felt it if there were that many souls in that house."

"Perhaps. If they were all in the house at once. My source tells me that the Indrori seems to be able to move in and out of places, separating souls and joining them together at will."

I rolled my eyes. "Well, forgive me if I don't trust your source. I'm in this field, Mr. Bishop. I know what spirits are capable of. And what you're talking about is impossible."

"My source also tells me that there was a breach in the Infernum not too long ago."

I raised an eyebrow. *The Infernum?* It sounded like a nightclub, but somehow, I knew if I said that, he'd be Mr. Grumpy Pants with me, so I let him continue. He seemed to like to hear himself talk. Hell, I did, too.

"It's a prison, of sorts, for immortals, and also home to some not-so-friendly ghosts," he clarified.

"Let me guess, these hundred or so spirits did the breaching?" I said, waiting for the punchline.

"Not necessarily. We don't know how many may have escaped, but there was most definitely a massive energy shift in our town."

"I think it may be time you lay off the wacky tobacky, Roman."

My comment made no impact on his deadpan expression.

"Fine. Don't accept my information, but don't expect to recover your partner without it."

I glared at him. He had me by the short hairs, and he knew it.

"Tick-tock, Tasha," he replied. Though his tough exterior showed he was firmly in control of the situation, there was an edge to his eyes. A pleading, almost. In spite of his confidence, I got the distinct sense that he needed my help just as much as I needed his.

"Fine. Tell me what you know."

His lips curled into a smile. "That's a good girl."

CHAPTER 7

$\mathcal{F}$orty minutes later, I had heard everything about Havenwood Falls and the thing that was living in that house. What he told me left my mouth hanging open, and not in the good way.

This entire town was made up of supernatural creatures and humans alike, all of them intermingling with each other as if nothing were out of the ordinary. One of the waitresses in this coffee shop, for example, was a witch, but the manager I flirted with was a human. The owner of the shop was a fae. Naturally.

"What kind are you?" I asked Roman when I was able to form semi-coherent thoughts.

Roman leaned across the table, waving his hand around almost like he was trying to swat away a fly, and then clasped his hands in front of him.

"I am a warlock."

"Naturally," I said, though nothing about him being a witch was natural at all! I eyed him again and reconsidered his hand movement.

"Did you just cast a spell?"

His eyes narrowed.

"I merely muffled our conversation from prying ears," he said, as though that were the most natural thing on the planet.

"How are the people—humans, I should say—not freaked out that they are next door neighbors with a vampire, or shifter, or whatever the hell might want to eat them for dinner?"

"That would never happen. The Court of the Sun and the Moon, the true governing body of Havenwood Falls, ensures things don't get out of hand, and we don't end up eating each other. Well, much. The Court knows all. Sees all. Yes, Tasha, even you will get a visit from them, soon enough. Well, besides me, that is."

"Me? Why?" I didn't like the sound of people keeping tabs on me. Especially in a place like this, where there might be eyes everywhere.

"Like I said, we keep tabs on everyone and everything. Especially the tourists. Plus, we have magical wards and protections in place. That really isn't your concern at the moment. Taking care of this Indrori is. You are the only one who can fix this."

"You keep saying that, but you don't seem to comprehend my point. Yes, I'm the best in my field, but what you're asking me to do is impossible. Not with the equipment I have," I repeated for the third time since he told me about the Indrori. I was like a broken record he refused to listen to.

He stood up, buttoned his suit jacket, and slid his coat on.

"Ultimately, the choice is yours, Tasha. Try my plan, as outlined, and bring your partner back to this realm, or leave altogether. But I can guarantee you this: nobody will save your partner if you choose to leave. Our town is currently up against a formidable force that this Indrori may be just one small part of, and saving all of the people of this town comes before one person nobody even knows is here." With that, he took one final sip from his mug, pulled a fifty-dollar bill from his wallet, and tossed it on the table before he left me alone to consider my options.

Eduardo came back in as soon as Roman left. He'd been watching our discussion from outside like a hawk ready to pounce if he tried anything funny. It would have been a sweet display of jealousy if we weren't so royally fucked.

"So? What was that all about?" he asked as a few new people entered the shop. They were happily chatting with each other, warming their fingers with hands cupped to their mouths. Completely oblivious to the hell that lived a few blocks away.

I stood up. "Not here. We've got eyes."

I glanced over to Davis, who was chatting with his new customers. How much did he know about the town he lived in? Was he one of them? Or was he one of the poor saps left in the dark?

Spooked, I put on my coat. Eduardo nodded once, and we left Coffee Haven. We walked toward the center of the town square. I ignored the blast of cold air hitting me from all angles, suddenly unable to feel the chill against my skin. It was all I could do not to throat punch the kids on the corner singing Christmas carols.

"Tasha, slow down. Talk to me. What did that asshat say to you?"

I slowed my pace and stood in front of the fountain. My eyes glassed over a bit.

"Did you ever read any fantasy books when you were a kid?" I asked, still trying to process everything Roman told me.

Eduardo looked at me funny, but answered me anyway. "Do comic books count?"

I nodded, though my mind was a million miles away.

His hand caught my shoulder, forcing my mind to stop spinning.

"Tasha, what's all this about? What did he say that has you so rattled?"

"It's all real," I whispered, focusing on the fountain a few feet away. "All of it. Vampires, witches, shifters. It's not just ghosts that walk among us. There really are terrible things that go bump in the night." I wasn't so sure why it was such a leap to believe in all the rest, when I knew full well that ghosts were real. But I'd grown up seeing ghosts. Today was the first time that I'd ever spoken to a witch . . . that I was aware of, anyway.

"What are you talking about? Babe, you're freaking me out."

I stood and watched the fountain, which was still running even in this weather. I tilted my head as I watched what looked like flecks of something shiny in the water. I took a step closer to be sure I was really seeing what I saw. Of course they had a fountain that rained gold.

Hell, the water probably wasn't even water. It was probably unicorn tears.

"There's no time to explain it all right now, but," I said, shaking my head, "I know what took Adam."

Eduardo stiffened. "What are we up against?"

"Something we've never trapped before. A super spirit of sorts called the Indrori," I said, as I turned away from the fountain and headed back toward the house. "So we have to hurry."

The sun was starting to set as we raced back to the house. It cast an eerie shadow across everything the darkness touched. The last thing I wanted to do was go back into that house again, especially now that I knew what I was up against, but Roman's plan was just crazy enough to work. I had to try, for Adam's sake.

Eduardo ran after me, quickly matching my stride.

"Tasha, what the hell is an Indrori?"

"According to Roman—"

"Since when are you on a first name basis with our contact?" There was no mistaking the jealousy in his tone. This was not the time to have this discussion.

I needed him to follow orders. "He's not FBI. We were tricked into coming here because of our unique skill set—well, *my* skill set. Roman is one of the guys in charge of this town. He seems to think I'm the only person who can defeat this thing and save Adam."

"What, you wanna go back in there?"

I nodded. "I have to, Eduardo. According to Roman, the Indrori is like a ghost cluster. One soul absorbing the spirits around him."

"Like that case in Sweden?" he asked.

"Yeah, except this one can manage more than a few spirits. Over a hundred. And possibly one more, now that he has Adam."

Eduardo stopped walking for a second.

"Hold up. Since when can a ghost absorb that many spirits?"

"Since about four hundred years ago. Apparently, there are legends of such a beast existing that far back. There was a mass breakout from the prison that held all these spirits. That's when we got the call." My feet were flying back to the house as fast as my words were coming out of my lips. I had a plan, a long shot at best, but it just might save Adam, if I hurried.

"Tasha, wait up," Eduardo yelled, catching up with me. I was on a mission. I needed to get back to the house.

"What prison?"

I stopped walking and faced Eduardo.

"Look, there isn't time to repeat everything Roman told me. Just trust me on this; we are up against the most powerful thing I've ever seen. There are five traps to go up against hundreds. Every second I waste explaining how any of this is possible is a second we lose trying to save Adam."

"What's your plan then? Just bust in there, traps blazing, and hope for the best?" he fumed. I knew he was frustrated. I was too, but there just wasn't time.

I started walking again. "No. I'm going to use myself as bait."

A moment later, he was at my side again. I pulled out a bottle of pills from my pocket.

"What are those?" He reached for the bottle, but I shoved them back inside and continued walking.

"Roman gave them to me. They're placebo sleeping pills. When I get back to the house, I'm going to pretend to be exhausted and pop a few of these to 'nap' alongside Adam. He says they won't be able to resist such a good target. They'll merge into one, and when the fuckers get close to me, I'll bag 'em."

"Tasha, will you stop for one second? Jesus!"

Exasperated, I spun around.

"What?" I snapped.

"You aren't thinking rationally. You just told me that we're up against a demonic coven all rolled into one mega badass boss and you just want to waltz in there with a weapon that has no hope of bringing that many spirits down?"

"First off, *we* aren't doing anything. You're no longer on the mission. Not one foot back in there. Do you understand?" He started to protest, and I held up a finger. "That's an order. You are powerless against what's inside. You can't see them like I can. You won't be able to escape if they come for you, and I'm not risking you being taken, too." I could see his macho-man argument coming, so I tried to soften my tone. I ran my hand across the side of his face. "I can't lose you, Eduardo. I don't know if I'll be able to get Adam back, but I won't risk you. I won't. You are not to step one toe on that property."

"So what am I supposed to do? Just wait outside?" Eduardo was clearly pissed. I'd never taken him off a mission before.

"No. You're going home. Go back to Coffee Haven. Roman has arranged for the bus to pick you up and drop you at the airport. Your ticket info should be in your email soon."

"This is bullshit, Tasha. I won't leave you."

I took his hand, defusing his anger, and pressed my lips against his gently. "You will, because this is a direct order. Go. Now."

His expression changed when he heard the pleading in my voice. It was a manipulative tactic, sure, but one I had to use. The only way to get him to safety was to make him believe he had my heart. I couldn't help it if he was foolish enough to believe I had one to give.

Leaning in, I gave him one final kiss and walked away. Eduardo didn't follow me, as I knew he wouldn't. He wouldn't disobey an order, even one as impossible as the one I'd given. He was a soldier first and foremost, and I used that to my ultimate advantage. This was between me and the shitstorm waiting for me back at the house.

Reaching into my jacket, I touched the pills again, clutching the bottle in my hand as I went over the plan in my mind. Once I rounded this block, I'd have to pretend that nothing was amiss. I needed to go back inside, cool as a cucumber, and act like Adam was still sleeping, and then quickly join him.

One nagging problem was that I had no idea how they had taken down Adam so fast. Normally, a demonic spirit attacked only at night when we were at our weakest. Even then, it's a bite or claw mark. They sucked Adam's entire soul out in a matter of seconds in full daylight and with Eduardo in the next room! Then again, we'd never dealt with this many souls all at once. Apparently, they could do things I couldn't even fathom.

The hardest part of the plan would be sneaking a trap into the bed with me before they tried to attack, but I had something in mind for that. These assholes may be able to merge into one supreme being, but there was one thing I had that no one could resist, dead or alive.

Back at the house, I unlocked the door and let myself in, humming lightly as I did.

"Adam? You up yet?" I asked, closing the door behind me. Three red spirits entered through the walls to watch me. "I'm afraid we've lost our son to the slopes," I said, faking a laugh. "Although it may have been the snow bunnies he was interested in more than the trails." I reached into my jacket pocket and grabbed the pills, then threw the coat onto the couch. I aimed it directly at a spirit, who didn't move as it came down on him. The jacket worked its way through him like a cloud of smoke, my phone spilling out on the cushion next to it. A moment later the spirit had reformed. That was not good. Spirits I was familiar with usually took hours to reshape themselves when disturbed like that. This one did it in a matter of seconds. These guys were strong. Far stronger than I had anticipated.

Trying to steady my nerves, I ventured up the stairs as fast as I could without actually running. Clearing the landing, I made my way into the bedroom with my red shadows following close behind. In the hall, I was joined by two others.

"I told him to have fun, and I was gonna come back to the house and," I walked in to discover Adam still flat on his back, "pass out." I chuckled, keeping my disguise up.

I glanced at the clock beside him. Almost two hours had gone by. Fuck. I had to work fast.

"Napping sounds like a great idea," I whispered. Adam's bag, which held one of my traps, was at the foot of the bed. "But first, a shower."

Grabbing the bag, I went into the bathroom. I could feel the spirits following me. A total of eight now, by my count. The ruse of a shower had worked. There was an eagerness in the air that hadn't been there before. Spirits, much like humans, were horny things for the most part, and I was counting on that for my plan to work. My body was going to have to be my ace in the hole.

Closing the bathroom door, I opened the bag, thankful to find two of my traps waiting. Each was about the size of a gun with a rectangular barrel. The only way out of this was to get them to combine. One shot to take down many. I might not get them all, but I had five tries to take down as many as I could. It might bag enough to drag Adam out of the house before they could stop me. It was a long shot, but I had to try. I wasn't going to leave a member of my crew behind.

Hence the shower. I needed them distracted. I wanted their eyes on my assets, not the sleight of hand trick I planned to play on them. Emboldened, I walked over to the shower, which had a glass door. Perfect. Turning the water on, I unbuttoned my blouse, one button at a time, feeling the energy in the room shift. I swore half of the demonic spirits I caught were just sexually frustrated auras. They had nowhere to put that much pent-up energy, so they took it out on the humans they were stuck living with. I planned to use their frustration today to my advantage.

As the water warmed, I removed the elastic band that held my French braid in place, working my fingers slowly through my hair to release it into black ribbons down my back. Shrugging out of my shirt, I kicked off my heels as my blouse fell to the floor. I shimmied out of my pants, leaving me only in my black lace bra and panties. They were watching me, and they were pleased.

Might as well give them the full show.

Unhooking my bra, I let it fall next to my blouse and then pulled down my panties slowly, making sure to give them the best view as I bent at the waist to take them off.

Sliding open the shower door, I stepped inside, letting the water saturate my hair and run down my back. Through half-closed eyes, I saw the spirits draw nearer to take in my fully exposed body. So far, so good.

I took as quick a shower as possible. I was well aware that Adam was waiting. I had to work fast. Turning the water off, I grabbed a towel and dried off my hair. Letting the rest of the water trickle down my naked body, I walked over to the bag. Time to make my move.

This was Adam's travel bag, so the traps were mixed in with his clothing, for reasons just like this. I dug around inside until I found one of Adam's T-shirts. Perfect.

I yanked the white shirt over my still wet body. Though the view was now obscured, the shirt clung to my damp skin. *Eyes on the peep show, boys.* Flipping my head upside down as though to finish drying it, I positioned the towel over the bag and "accidentally" dropped it directly over the trap. A moment later, I picked up the towel, with the neatly hidden trap nestled safely inside it. Step one done.

I made my way to the bed with the towel at my side as though I was merely bringing the towel with me to finish drying off my hair. I placed the bundle on the pillow next to Adam and then went back to retrieve the sleeping pills from the bathroom.

"I am dead tired. I hope these sleeping pills help make up for the jet lag," I whispered to myself, but loud enough for the spirits to hear. I popped open the cap and swallowed a handful, dry. I tried not to gag as they went down. I'd assumed they'd taste more like sugar than sand paper.

As the placebos worked their way down my throat like mini razor blades, I tucked the trap under my pillow, then finished towel-drying my hair. I faked a yawn, tossed the towel to the floor, and pulled the sheets over me. I turned onto my side, away from Adam and facing the spirits. One hand over the top of the sheets, one hand under the pillow. My finger on the trigger.

Come on, you dirty bastards. Join up so I can knock you all out at once. If Roman was right, there was a very good chance not all of the spirits were even here. His theory was that the Indrori moved around and absorbed souls at will, so if I could take out these eight, it might buy me enough time to recover Adam and get the hell out of dodge. Screw Havenwood Falls. They could find someone more qualified than me to take on this mess. My priority was Adam. Being bait to save him would be worth it.

Any second now . . .

The tick of the clock went by painfully slowly. Each second sounded like a drum in my ears. Twenty minutes of trying to keep one eye slightly open was mentally exhausting. Remaining motionless proved easier, however, the longer I lay there. I was growing anxious, ready for them to merge. *When were they going to strike?*

After thirty minutes, I had to shut my eyelid because it started to flutter, which would give me away, but before I did, I saw one of the red spirits disappear. *Finally!* They were merging.

My finger was still on the trigger as I waited. In the warm cocoon of the duvet, I inadvertently let out a large yawn. I chided myself for allowing it to escape, but so far, the spirits hadn't backed off. In fact, I swore they merged again, because there was a definite shift in the temperature. When a second yawn ripped through me, however, a slow onset of panic set in.

I tried to open my eyes, but I couldn't. They were heavy. Like lead. In fact, my whole body felt numb. My head swam like it was drifting in and out of consciousness. I could no longer feel my finger on the trap. I couldn't feel any part of my body.

All at once, reality came crashing down. Roman hadn't given me placebos. I'd been given the real deal. He set me up.

I tried to remember how many I'd swallowed. A few I could probably fight, but I easily took six or seven, maybe more. What had it mattered? They were supposed to be fakes. Jesus. *Why would Roman do this to me?*

My mind spun as I felt the temperature of the room turn to ice. That could only mean one thing. More had arrived. Paralyzed by the sleeping pills, I could do nothing now. I was helpless. I was the one who was trapped and about to be taken into the spirit realm.

CHAPTER 8

I had been told countless times what it was like to die by the souls I'd managed to recover over the years. The stories were so similar that I knew their accounts must have had at least some shred of truth to them. Even with all that knowledge of existence beyond the living, I was still not prepared for what I saw.

The transition began on my lips, like a kiss from a lover who had been out in the cold. The chill then webbed slowly across my face, giving me the sensation of having my head submerged under icy water. All warmth drained away as the feeling traveled down my neck, then spread out to each arm. I was conscious, suddenly, only of the heat within my toes, curled tight under the sheets, until they too succumbed to the pull of the spirit realm.

When I opened my eyes anew, it was with the eyes of a ghost. I had been taken to the other side of the living. Just as Adam had been.

Turning my head around, I could tell that I was still in the house, but everything was dark and blurry, as though I were stuck in dense fog. Looking down at my body, I noticed that it still looked like me, except for one key difference. I was translucent. That actually brought me comfort. It meant I wasn't dead. Not fully. Not yet. If I was a full spirit, the edges of my form wouldn't be quite so defined. I would appear more blob-like.

I was between worlds, so my physical body was still on the bed, while my aura lay trapped here. Wherever here was. I was on the clock now, too. Only now, there was no one around to help.

Think, Tasha. Who else could help Adam and me? That, by far, would be the largest hurdle. There were only a handful of people on the planet who recovered souls, and as far as I knew, not a single one was in the United States. The FBI intentionally spread us out on each continent, save for Antarctica, because anyone stupid enough to go there deserved what they got. It made sense logically to be spread out, so we could make sure a Recoverer could arrive at any place around the globe within hours, since time was essential in recovering a soul. However, that also meant the others wouldn't be able to get to Adam and me in time, even if they knew where we were, which they didn't.

That realization hit me like a wall. No one knew where we were. Roman had tricked my team into coming here, so my division had no idea I was even in Colorado, much less trapped in purgatory. Plus, I was scheduled for a vacation anyway, so they wouldn't come looking for me for at least a week, which would be too late. I'd sent Eduardo away, which meant the only person who knew about our situation was the one person who had sent us here. Roman Bishop.

I cursed. We were screwed. Getting us out of here alive was entirely up to me. How, I had no idea. The first thing I needed to do was to find Adam. Maybe he had an idea. After all, he was the logistical one of the team. He'd had a lot more time to think about our situation than I had.

Spinning around, I realized that my movements in this reality were effortless. I looked down and noticed that my feet no longer touched the ground, but hovered about an inch above it instead. This helped to confirm that I wasn't fully dead yet. If I was a true ghost, my movements would be coming harder and slower than this. While I continued to exist in both worlds, it seemed I would retain the physical properties of both realms. It was my only advantage that I could see. As the hours ticked on, however, my ability to move would likely be reduced. This was the sort of problem Adam would love to solve. I had to find him.

Floating around the bed, I searched for any sign of him. While I knew he was on the bed in the human world, here in the spirit world, the bed beside me was empty. He had either moved or had been taken elsewhere.

"Adam!" The sound that came from my throat sounded foreign against my lips. It was more like a moan than an articulated word. I called out his name again around a tongue that was having a hard time making the right noises.

As I floated through the room, I noticed that, while I wasn't completely see-through yet, my aura did have a light blue tinge to it. The aura of a confused spirit. Talk about hitting the nail on the head. Not only was I confused about my actual state of existence, I was confused about how I planned on getting back. I had no traps, no game plan, and absolutely zero clue of how to escape.

Wait. I did have traps. They were in this very bedroom.

Determined, I floated toward the pillow I'd hidden the trap under. When I tried to lift the pillow up, however, my hand disappeared straight through it.

"Shit!" I hissed. My voice came out slow, like maple syrup. I should have known I wouldn't be able to manipulate objects here. From my understanding, it took spirits years before they could so much as move a lace curtain, and I was trying to pick up a heavy trap?

An overwhelming sense of dread filled me. I didn't know what to do. I was in a different world, and I didn't know the rules. How was I going to get out of here if I didn't fully understand where *here* was?

That's when I heard a moan that wasn't mine. A voice that was deep and low but laced with agony.

"Adam?"

I floated down the hall, searching for where the sound was, checking the second bedroom and bathroom. I found nothing but dark corners. The cry came again, and this time, I could tell it was coming from below me. I made my way down the stairs and into the living area.

Heading downstairs was harder than I expected. I had to focus hard to move downward versus just hovering straight across the stairwell. It was maddening not being able to get to him faster. When I finally figured out how to point my aura in the direction I wanted to go, I rushed into the living room.

Gone was the bright sun and winter landscape from the bay windows of this morning, and in its place was more darkness. There were no street lamps, no Christmas decorations glowing from neighboring houses. The only thing that stood out in the shadows was a faint blue glow coming from the far corner of the room. It was Adam.

The second I made a move to go toward him, however, the color of the room shifted. Through the floorboards, a deep purple haze seeped through the cracks. Instantly, my training kicked in, suspecting a nerve gas attack, but then I stopped myself. *Nerve gas wouldn't do anything to a spirit.*

With my guard up, I watched as the fog continued to enter the room, this time from every angle—through the walls, around the window frames, down from the ceiling. The smoke converged into one centralized area directly in front of Adam.

I knew, without any shadow of a doubt, that this was the Indrori. In silent awe, I watched the sheer size and color of this thing as it formed into one giant mass. It was unlike anything I had ever encountered in all my years as a Spirit Agent. The color too—dark purple, ominous and chilling—was unlike anything I'd ever seen before. The smoke began to swirl around Adam like a vortex.

"Leave him alone!" I shouted, although the sound that came out was surprisingly weak.

The Indrori did nothing to stop the descent on Adam, so I rushed over in my useless form, ready to fight. When our auras connected, however, I felt the true power of the Indrori. In an instant, I was knocked backward, clear across the room, as though an explosion had gone off. My side actually felt like a shard of metal had pierced me.

The vortex stopped spinning around Adam and changed course—toward me. I held my hands over my head in a feeble attempt to ward the beast off.

"I knew you were a fighter, Agent Young, but I didn't expect you to be foolish as well."

I whipped my head up, realizing that thing had just called me by my name. It knew who I was.

The voice of it was neither male nor female, but somehow a combination of both. The Indrori was communicating with me, but not through any mouth that I could make out. In fact, there was nothing resembling a human form, save for vague skull-like shapes that danced within the smoke. This, more than anything else, confirmed for me that there was definitely more than one soul inside him. There were too many skulls for me to count as they swirled in and out of the smoke.

"Leave him alone," I said again, barely able to see Adam's aura through the Indrori's.

"Or what? You'll swat at me again?" The ripple of different people's laughter danced around the room.

"Take me instead," I shouted. "Let him go and take me!"

"Oh, such chivalry for the man you're not even screwing. I would have thought you'd save that loyalty for the one you are. Where is the boy-toy, Eduardo, by the way? And don't lie to us again and say he's skiing."

"How . . ." I couldn't even form the sentence. *How would the Indrori possibly know about my relationship with Eduardo?* We'd only used our cover stories at the house. How could the Indrori know we were more intimate?

"Oh, Tasha, we know everything about you. Right down to the way you like to be fucked."

My mouth opened to speak, but I couldn't find the words. The confidence with which it spoke made me believe it knew that and more.

"We have been watching you since your birth," It said. "One or more of us have been following your journey very carefully."

They had been stalking me. That wasn't at all freaky.

"Why?"

"Why? Oh, come now, Agent Young, surely you know why the

spirit world would be interested in you." The voices echoed around me in chorus.

Despite my very unstable situation, I found myself getting defensive. The work I did was noble, when you got right down to it. I was helping rid the world of harmful spirits.

"Look, I don't know what your problem is, but whatever it is, it's with me, not my partner. Now let him go."

Laughter filled the room. It came from every side, like a souped-up version of surround sound, except this really was all around me.

"You honestly don't know why we have a problem with you?" They asked. "You, a being who has the ability to eradicate our very existence? You who, with a simple pull of a trigger, can destroy decades' worth of work a spirit fought for? You can't fathom why we might take a vested interest in you?"

The truth was becoming uncomfortably clear.

"Agent Young, you, and those like you, are creating the genocide of my kind, and you mean to tell me that you don't understand why we want the problem eliminated?"

And there it was. My crime laid out. I was the ghost world's Hitler, and they wanted to end me.

The only trouble was I saw no way to prevent the Indrori from doing just that.

CHAPTER 9

The Indrori moved as one giant mass as it circled me from all sides. I could feel the hatred from the spirits within pouring onto me. They wanted to finish the job they started by removing my soul from my body. To a human, the worst they could do as a demonic spirit was leave a few claw marks on the flesh. Together, as one united form, however, they had enough combined energy to literally remove my soul from my still-living body. It left me vulnerable to whatever torment they had in mind next.

"Stop!" Adam's barely audible voice said from behind the Indrori.

"He's taking a rather long time to die, don't you think?" The Indrori sighed. "It's been annoying listening to him whine, but we needed a reason for you to stick around and not run away. We knew you wouldn't be able to resist saving your partner. Even if it meant sacrificing yourself to get here."

Wait. They think I came up with the plan to be taken on my own? Does that mean Roman isn't working with them?

"Now that you are finally here, however, we have no need for your partner."

The Indrori's energy left me then and began to swarm around Adam.

"No! Stop. Your issue is with me!" I shouted. "Take me instead."

At that, the Indrori paused. "All in due time, Agent Young."

The purple haze grew thick and dark as it circled Adam. There was one scream of agony from his lips, then it was cut off. The mist from the Indrori flowed into Adam's aura until it dissolved into the dark violaceous haze of the Indrori. In a matter of seconds, Adam was no more.

"No!" I screamed, but even as my lips parted to make the words come out, I knew it was too late. Adam's soul had been consumed by the Indrori.

"What are you waiting for?" I cried. "You brought me here; you've eliminated anyone who could have helped me escape. Just kill me already!"

They seemed to be dragging this out. Likely to make me suffer. Assholes.

"All in due time, Tasha. For now, I must rest. One does get full after a big meal, doesn't one?" Their laughter surrounded me again.

Just like that, the dark cloud around me dissipated and drifted back through the cracks from which they came. For a moment, I didn't move. I thought their disappearance was a trap somehow, but I didn't feel them anywhere in the house. They really had left me alone.

Time was not on my side. I had to find a way out of this house and fast. I had no idea how long of a "rest" he would need before coming back for me, so I needed to escape while I could.

In my semi-transparent state, however, doing anything fast was problematic. Since I didn't have feet that touched the floor, the only way to move was to float, and I had yet to figure out the speed control in this plane, which was maddening all on its own.

Logically, the first place to try was the front door. I had no idea what I'd do once outside, but I couldn't just wait around and be a sitting duck. Maybe I could find Roman and haunt him or something until he figured out a way to help me.

When my hand reached for the door, however, the handle didn't budge because my hand went right through it. Of course it did.

"Fuck. Okay. That's fine. I don't need to use a door. I'm a ghost now. I can float through shit."

Closing my eyes, I moved toward the door, and to my delight, my body easily manifested itself outside as though there was nothing in my way at all. First there was a door, and then, when I opened my eyes, there wasn't.

"Cool."

There was an intense feeling of relief that I was no longer inside the darkness of the house, even if the outside looked just as dark as the inside. I wasn't sure if that was because it was night or if everything in the spirit world was dark.

The first logical thing I needed to do was find a way to reach Eduardo. Maybe the bus hadn't picked him up yet? If he was still around, he could reach out to the Bureau and try to get a Recoverer here in time. I had no idea if I would be able to make a journey that far away, though I had to try. A six-minute walk was nothing for a human, but light-years for a spirit.

When I tried to float down the sanded walkway, however, I discovered that I was unable to move any farther. It felt like I was caught on something.

Glancing behind me, I saw that my lower half was still stuck inside the house. I was half in and half out.

"What the fuck?"

I tried moving forward, but my aura did not come out any farther.

"Shit."

I was tethered to the house.

I chided myself for thinking that because I was only a half spirit, the rules wouldn't apply to me. It was only ancient and demonic souls that had found a way to merge outside of the space they died in. Even then, it wasn't more than a few hundred feet, which meant that wherever the Indrori went, he wouldn't be that far away. That's why he had no issue with leaving me unguarded. He knew I would still be trapped.

Yet I refused to believe that I was helpless. There had to be something I could do. Some way to make the traps work. Some weakness the Indrori had that I could take advantage of. I couldn't be a sitting duck. I just couldn't be.

A wave of rage swept over me as I screamed into my prison.

"Hey, Universe! I could use some fucking help here!" I shouted to no one in particular. I was a firm believer in karma and evil always losing, but right now that picture wasn't looking so good. "Do you hear me, world? I need help!"

"Stop shouting already. I can hear you, Jeez Louise!"

My head whipped around, trying to find where the female voice came from. Was the Indrori back? If so, why was it only one voice I could hear?

"Who's there?"

"My name is Harper Sinclair. I'm a spiritual scribe. You called out for help. Here I am." The girl's voice sounded bored. Like she's said this speech a hundred times before. *"Wait. Who are you? You don't sound like a demonic spirit."*

"A spiritual what? And demonic? Where the fuck are you?" I floated from room to room, trying to figure out where the voice was coming from. I refused to believe it was coming from my own mind. Was this a trick of the Indrori?

"My location doesn't matter. Look, I'm just trying to help. If you're not a demonic spirit, you must be damn close to one, because that's the only kind of spirit I can talk to. Unless you're an angel. Are you?"

She thought I was a demonic spirit, or worse, an angel. That must mean she was human, and a psychic of some kind.

"Look, I'm no angel. And I'm not a ghost, either. Not fully anyway. I'm a human." I looked down at my figure, well, through it. "Sort of. It's complicated. Where are you right now?"

I could hear her exasperation in my mind.

"If you must know, I'm in the woods and was about to take a picture of a nesting red-tailed hawk, but you keep shouting in my head, which is super weird and uber annoying. I've never actually heard anyone before, not like this. My abilities have never worked like this. You are kind of freaking me out. So can you tell me what the heck is going on?"

I decided it mattered little that I couldn't see this voice or that I had no idea what a psychic scribe was. At the moment, she was the only thing around that might help me figure this mess out. I'd asked the universe for help, and this was what it gave me. I was going with it.

For the next several minutes, I tried to explain, as succinctly as I could, the events of the last few hours, which even I was having a hard time believing.

"*Wait. You're up against an Indrori?*" came Harper's stunned reply when I had finished.

"Yeah," I said, relieved that she seemed to know what I was up against. "What do you know about the Indrori?"

"*I'm the one it contacted first. I told the Court about it as soon as it happened. Are you Tasha Young?*"

"The one and only." This Harper must have been the source Roman kept referring to. "Great. So we're on the same page. How the hell do I defeat it?"

There was no answer to my question, which I didn't take as a good sign. Surely, if there had been an easy way to do it, she would have rattled it off just to be done with me.

"Harper? What do I do?" Still no answer. "Harper?"

Great. She probably knew I was a goner.

"*Sorry. I'm back. I needed to get another journal. I tore through the last one.*"

"A journal? Why do you need a journal? Are you writing down my final words or something?"

"*No,*" she said. Her voice felt rushed. "*It's a long story, but it's how I communicate with the other side. By writing. Usually, I talk and the spirits answer through writing. You are different. This is backwards for me. Maybe because of where you are. Are you . . . dead?*"

"No, I'm not dead," I said with more conviction than I felt. I *wasn't* dead . . . yet.

"*Of course. Sorry. I don't really understand the logistics of how we are talking right now. This is all very strange for me,*" she apologized.

"You and me both, kid." Though I had no idea what Harper looked like, I sensed she was young. I was guessing early to mid-twenties. My entire fate rested on a girl who spoke to spirits with a pen. I was fucked.

"Tasha, listen to me very carefully. I need to know where you are right now."

"I'm in the house hiding from that thing!"

Harper's voice became agitated. *"You're inside the actual house on Thirteenth? The big green one? Alone?"*

"Yeah. That's where Roman sent me."

"This was not the plan. I'm on my way!"

At those words, a reckless plan formulated in my head. I could teach her how to use the traps. So what if no one but me had ever been able to use them successfully before? I'd be right beside her. I could tell her where to aim it. It was an option. The only one I had.

"Oh, and Tasha, try to stay hidden as best you can, though up against an Indrori that's kind of impossible," Harper added.

"Gee, thanks for the vote of confidence."

"This is no joke," Harper warned. *"I got a glimpse of this Indrori when it first reached out, and it's nothing like the other demons and spirits I've worked with. I don't know how the hell you ended up there alone, but I need to let the Court know. We'll need backup, for sure."*

"I'm not so sure they would help, considering one of their own set me up. That rat, Roman Bishop, is the one who drugged me," I spat. If I got out of this, his was the first neck I was gonna wring.

"That makes no sense. Sure, the Bishop boys like to stir up trouble, but this is insane, even for them. Look, let me handle that. You just stay hidden."

Her voice sounded so small against the enormity of the situation.

"Thanks, kid. Hope to see you soon."

Just like that, the connection I had with Harper was severed. It felt about the same as a door being shut in my face.

Still, there was good news. Harper was on the way. Possibly with backup from the Court. What a bunch of suits were going to do I had no idea, but then, nothing about Havenwood Falls made much sense.

For the moment, there was hope. I clung to that small shot in the dark as tightly as I did to the sliver of my humanity.

CHAPTER 10

J tried not to count the seconds since I last spoke with
Harper. Just like I tried not to jump at every sound I heard.
So far, I was failing on both counts. The Indrori could be back any
time, and without Harper, there was no hope of escape. I was a mouse
in a cage, waiting for the snake to pounce.

My fingers ran absently along my waist to where my own snake
tattoo was. I could almost feel it wrapping tighter around me,
squeezing the life from me . . . much like the Indrori wanted to do.

I had no idea how big Havenwood Falls really was or where
Harper was coming from within it. I was banking on her arriving in
enough time for me to teach her how to use the trap before our giant
purple people eater came back to dine on my soul.

"Please, God, if you're listening . . . Thanks for sending Harper . . .
Now, if you get me out of this mess, I'll . . . stop drinking. No. I won't.
You and I both know that's a lie. Um, I'll stop sleeping around. As
much," I amended.

That's when I heard a noise. A telltale ringing of my cell phone.
Was God calling me on my cell? Curious, I went back inside and into
the living room, where I saw it on the couch, face up, where it had
fallen out when I ditched my coat before I was forcibly removed from
my flesh.

It wasn't God. It was Eduardo. Instinctively, I went to pick it up, but, of course, my fingers went right through the cell and into the couch beneath it.

"Damn it!" What a frustrating place to be in. I was utterly useless and defenseless.

Because the phone was face up, I could at least read the text message.

Eduardo: You know, the guys all warned me. They told me you'd burn my ass. I was convinced I was gonna be the one to change that. Guess I was just another notch on your belt, huh?

I stared at the words illuminated on my screen, hating the truth behind them. While I hadn't quite finished playing with Eduardo, I would have sent him packing soon enough. After a while, I cut them all loose. So why did his words sting so much?

Eduardo: You could have just told me you were done with me, you know? I never took you to be a liar. That's cool. Whatever. Give my regards to Roman. And tell him to wear a hat.

Of course he thought he'd been dumped for Roman. He wasn't totally off. If I hadn't been in this current mess, I may have pursued Roman. I'd be pissed at myself for going after the bastard, but I probably would have.

Ugh. Roman. That slimy bastard. If I ever got out of this, I was gonna cut his dick off. He'd be lucky if I didn't do worse after he threw me in this trap. I didn't care what Harper thought. Roman was involved in this somehow. I just knew it.

"Tasha? You still alive?"

My head whipped around toward the front door. A female voice was calling out from behind it.

"Harper? Thank God."

I floated back through the door and got my first look at the person I had only been able to hear in my head. She wasn't at all like I was imagining, aside from the young part. That, I got right. She was in her early twenties, but she was way more casual than I had presumed. She had on jeans and a ratty old sweatshirt, which nearly swallowed up her petite frame. She wore her long brown hair tied back in a messy ponytail and had on massive hiker boots that looked two sizes too big.

When I looked back up, Harper was focused on a journal, writing something down. She didn't seem to notice me floating literally two inches in front of her.

"Tasha, where are you now? Is the Indrori back?" I saw her write on her pad.

"I'm fine. I'm standing right in front of you."

Harper looked up at me and stared right through me before she frowned.

"Ah, there you are. Sort of," she wrote. *"You're like a shadow."*

I nodded my head. "Well, I only see translucent-like auras in the spirit world, but I can see that you're solid. Guess that means you're still alive," I said.

Her eyebrows crinkled, and she went back to the journal. *For the moment.*

This was one bizarre conversation—me speaking and her writing—but I was more than thankful to have someone here who might be able to help me.

"So . . . what's the plan?" Harper asked.

"You come in, I show you how to use the spirit trap, we capture this jackass, and somehow get me home in the next four to five hours."

"What happens after five hours?"

"Oh, nothing major. Just that I can't come back to the land of the living after that. The brain doesn't function away from the soul after that long. So we're kind of on a clock here. Let's hope I didn't lock the door when I came in, or you'll have to break in."

"Right."

She tucked her journal under one arm and placed a hand on the door. If I had breath to hold, I would have as she turned the knob. Mercifully, it opened without issue.

"Finally, something goes my way," I said as Harper walked into the house. Her eyes were wide as she scanned the place, probably expecting to find the Indrori.

"How long do you think we have until it comes back?" I could hear

her fear inside my head. This wasn't fair, me dragging her into this. It wasn't her fight, but without her, I was defenseless. I wasn't able to save Adam, but I was going to make sure that Harper wasn't hurt. Somehow.

"The gun is in the bedroom. Through the living room, top of the stairs," I said, knowing we had little time to play with.

"Gun? You never mentioned a gun. You said trap. I don't know how to fire a gun!"

Her writing was shaky. I was freaking her out. I couldn't have her bolting on me. Not when I didn't have any other options.

"It *is* a trap. I shouldn't have said gun. Bad choice of words. It works sort of like a gun in that there is a trigger to pull, and I guess it's sort of shaped like a gun, but you won't be killing anyone with it."

I wasn't sure if I made it worse or better.

"Okay, right. I can't kill anyone because they are already dead." She bit her bottom lip as she looked down at the words.

I didn't mention that she could kill me if she didn't succeed, but that likely wouldn't help her nerves.

"Exactly. You'll trap the Indrori, and I'll bring them back to the feds, and we'll dispose of them properly."

Harper looked at me funny. *"Dispose of? You can't get rid of a demonic spirit. It's not possible. You have to send them back to Hell or the Infernum. It's the only safe place for a spirit as evil as the one after you."*

"'Cause that worked so great before."

"I know it's hard to believe it, but the Court will help make this right again."

"How long have you lived here?" I asked.

"I was born here," she said, putting down her pen and then holding up her wrist. On it was a tattoo of a writing quill. I nodded, remembering what Roman had told me about the town branding not only their supernatural people with magical tattoos, but their visitors, too. The quill seemed fitting for her power.

An errant thought slipped through my mind. What kind of tattoo would I get and where would I put it? I chided myself for the thought. A tattoo being placed on me required that my soul wasn't going to get sucked out *and* that it found a way to get back into my physical body. Two things that seemed beyond hope. At best, I could try to take this thing down so no one else would be taken, or at the very least, weaken it until someone from the Court could.

"In all seriousness, Harper, what makes you think this thing won't just break out again if we find a way to cage it again?"

"That's up to those with higher pay scales than us to figure out," Harper wrote. *"Getting them back there is going to be the tricky part. I can command demons, a few at a time, but I don't know if I'm strong enough to control that many spirits, so let's hope your trap works."*

"Control demons?" I asked. "You know what? I don't wanna know."

"So, this gun—trap thing—I just point it at the Indrori, and that's it?"

"Yeah, point and shoot," I said. It was a good thing she couldn't see my face, or she would have seen the lie there. It was a tad more complicated than that, but the less she knew about the odds of it working, the better. A nervous trigger finger didn't help anyone.

"The traps are up the stairs. In the bedroom, first door on the right."

Harper nodded and headed for the stairs. I followed her, trying to urge her along faster, but also trying not to freak her out.

"There should be one in the bag right near the bed," I instructed when she made it into the bedroom.

"Oh my god," Harper wrote, stopping once she saw the bed. She was looking at Adam's face-down, limp body. Mine was lying beside his.

"That's my partner. That thing under the covers beside him? That's me." It was weird seeing myself outside of my own skin. Though it was only a lump under a duvet, I knew if I pulled back the covers, I'd see my own lifeless body. "Adam is still alive, in that his organs are still functioning. He's breathing in and out . . . but his soul—" I fought back my emotion. It was still too hard to think about. "He's never going to come out of that vegetative state. They took his soul. The thing that made Adam, Adam." It was so hard to think I was never going to be able to talk to him again. "That's what is going to happen to me if the Indrori has his way."

"*Right. Let's not fail, okay?*" Her shoulders rose back as though she fully understood the stakes now.

Letting out a breath, Harper went over and unzipped the bag with ease. She lifted a trap up and shifted it to her other hand.

"*Wow, it's heavy,*" she scribbled with her right hand, as the trap remained in her left.

"Yeah, you're gonna want to grab a second one. One for each hand. Just to be safe."

Harper lowered the trap and looked in my general direction. Her eyes landed about a foot lower than where my eyes really were. A spot I was accustomed to men staring. She wasn't ogling me, even though her eyes were wide. She just didn't know how tall I was.

"*You think I'll need two of them?*"

I didn't have the heart to tell her she'd need to likely fire fifty of them at a time to take this thing down. That's when it hit me how big the stakes were for Harper. All this time, I'd been focusing on this being the only way to stop the Indrori, but what about her? I was sticking her in the same situation Roman had put me in. This was a bad idea. I couldn't do it. I wouldn't put her life on the line.

"You know what?" I said. "I've changed my mind. This is too dangerous. You need to get out of here before it comes back."

"*I'm not leaving you. I can help. I've been working with demons for almost a year now. Besides, I have these traps. I'm not some defenseless kid, Tasha. I can do this.*" She dropped her notepad to the ground, effectively cutting off our communication.

"Harper!" I shouted. "The plan won't work, okay? Even if you hit this thing dead in the center with both guns—it won't be enough. I was a fool to drag you into this. You need to get out of here before—"

At that moment, I felt a shift in the air. I knew Harper could feel it, if not see it too, because her posture stiffened.

"Get out of here. Now!" I hissed.

She stood there, like a deer stuck in headlights for a long moment. She held only one trap in her hand. Her entire body trembled as she lifted the gun toward the vibrant violet aura that merged its way into the bedroom from all around us.

"Sorry to keep you waiting, Agent Young," the Indrori began. "I had to make a quick trip to the bus stop. Couldn't let your boy-toy miss out on all the fun. He was delicious."

No. Eduardo. The fucker took him, too. He was tracking down anyone that was close to me.

"You bastard!" I shrieked. I felt my insides rattle against the pent-up rage. I was about to lurch for him when Harper shouted.

"Get out of the way! I got this!"

The Indrori shifted slightly to my left to take in Harper. The trap was raised between her two shaking hands.

"Agent Young, you brought me a snack. How delightful. But really, after devouring you, I'm not sure I could eat another bite." The laughter rose from the Indrori and reverberated across the room.

"Leave her out of this!" I yelled, essentially sealing her fate. It was a fatal slip of the tongue. I had just let the Indrori know who he should go after next.

"Harper, put the gun down and get out of here," I shouted at her. Couldn't she see how much danger she was in?

She ignored me and lifted the gun higher. Though she likely wouldn't be able to make out the exact shape of the Indrori as well I could, she must have seen its general direction, because the gun was pointed in the right spot. She closed her eyes and shot.

CHAPTER 11

*H*arper stood there, arm outstretched, eyes pinched tight, likely too afraid to open them to see the reality of the situation that I saw all too well. She had missed her mark by a mile.

"God damn it, Harper, run, now, or I'll kill you myself," I spat, at the exact same time as the Indrori moved in on her.

I forced my aura in front of the large mass. It halted as though amused.

"Rule number one: You don't get to touch my friends," I said.

"Friends? Oh, Agent Young, you don't have any friends." It was a childish retort. One that would have normally bounced right off me, but for some reason it stuck there like glue. The monster was right. I'd never had a friend. Not a genuine one. Ever since I discovered my gift as a child, people have only wanted what I could give them back—a loved one's life. I had gotten used to being used and, as a result, became suspicious of anyone who wanted to get close to me.

How could the Indrori know that I had always been a loner, though? Their tone indicated that they had intimate knowledge of my life.

"Tasha, get out of the way. I can handle this," Harper said. Her eyes were narrowed. Thin fingers danced through the air as though she were writing on an invisible sheet of paper. She was writing words that

I couldn't decipher, but it seemed to be doing something, because the room grew darker then. Shadows appeared from the corners, and I began to panic, thinking the Indrori was doing this.

"Foolish girl. You can't control us. One demonic soul, perhaps, but united, we are too strong for you."

Harper didn't seem deterred. She continued to write in the air as more shadows emerged. It was only then that I realized Harper was summoning the shadows.

"What are those, Harper?"

"Spirits," she grunted through her efforts. "I'm summoning them to help from the Infernum."

"Spirits? Harper, no! You can't—this thing *absorbs* spirits! You'll just make it stronger!"

"I've got control of them, Tasha," she strained. "Now stay back."

But it was clear to me that this was a losing battle. Already I could see violet tendrils reaching out to the dark shadows, wrapping themselves around the spirits Harper had summoned. Within moments, the shadows were gone, and the Indrori was even larger.

"Enough games!" the Indrori shouted. A wave of energy rocked through the room, bouncing Harper and me backward.

"Are you okay?" I asked. The energy blast had knocked her straight off her feet.

"It's too strong. I need to find Desi. I'll be back, Tasha. I'll bring help!"

A moment later, she was on her feet and bounding down the stairs. I didn't have time to ask her who Desi was, but I knew that whoever it was, it would be too late. There would be nothing left of me to save.

Scrambling to get my aura centered, I followed after Harper. I knew I couldn't escape the house, but I was stalling for time. I needed to think of something to do to weaken this bastard, and right now the only thing I could think of was trying to force it to use energy to chase after me. This was a game of cat and mouse that I didn't want to lose.

Downstairs I stopped in the living room. I heard the front door slam. Harper had made it out. That was a small comfort. Though we barely knew each other, I felt like we were friends. She hadn't wanted anything from me. In fact, I had been the one using her talent.

It didn't take long for the Indrori to drip down from the ceiling. The purple aura looked no worse for wear despite my efforts. Figures.

"Looks like it's just you and me now, *Beetlejuice*."

The thing was stronger than ever now, thanks to Harper's help. I had no idea how I was going to get out of this alive. The only thing I could think to do was try to stall for time. My mouth got me out of plenty of sticky situations. Maybe I'd find a way to talk myself free.

"Before you take my soul," I began, "I have a question or two."

The Indrori stopped its advancement toward me and hovered as though curious what I might want to know. I took it as permission to keep going.

"What's your end game? You take my soul and then what? Your revenge is over. Whatever will you do with your time? Off to the Bermuda Triangle, are you?"

"I'm disappointed, Tasha. I would have thought you had figured it out by now."

I didn't answer, because I didn't have a clue as to what he was getting at. He was playing a mind game. I just didn't know the rules. Still, I wanted to keep up the talking to give Harper as much time as I could to get far away from here.

Seemingly frustrated by my stupidity, his aura came closer. So close that I could feel his energy forcing itself against my own.

"You're the last of your kind, Tasha. The last Recoverer in the world."

I had no idea where he was getting his intel, but he was wrong. "No, I'm not. There are at least five of us, dipshit."

A small laughter surrounded me.

"Actually, there were six of you. *Were* being the operative word. Now, it's just you. Naturally, I saved the best for last. You are the end of an era."

"Bullshit," I hissed, but I couldn't help but wonder if they were right. I had no way of knowing if they were lying or not. Recoverers were so spread out, in different time zones. It's not like we kept in touch. We all had our own missions, but if they were all gone, surely, I would have heard something. Right?

I shook my head, blurring my aura as I did. I was fading. The Indrori's proximity was draining me.

"Fine, so you put an end to bringing back a few dead, so what? There are other spirit agents. We can still take you down!"

The Indrori split apart just then. Gone was the purple mass, in its place a sea of red with a few blue auras still clinging to what little humanity they had. I realized then, it was this combination of the demonic and the confused spirits that gave the Indrori its coloring.

"Your Spirit Agents can handle one of us at a time, Agent Young," the Indrori screamed, "but as one, we are unstoppable." A moment later, the auras were assembled again. Their power was in their numbers. I had to find a way to break them apart.

"Our teams are smart. They'll figure out a way to stop you."

More laughter. I was really getting sick of that sound.

"If they live long enough."

I couldn't help it. I let out a chuckle of my own. "What? You're going to take down every human spirit agent, too? There are literally thousands of us, with more being trained by the minute."

His reply came all at once, hot against my ear as if he was standing in the flesh beside me.

"You underestimate our power. We'll get every last human who wishes us harm. Once you are gone, there will be no one to stop us. After you, the endgame is simple. Every single person in Havenwood Falls. And then every single supernatural in this world, including the one known as the Collector. Their days of imprisoning our kind for merely existing are over."

Before I could react, their aura pulled away from mine as they circled what was left of my spirit in the same tornado-type motion they had done before they took Adam. I wasn't long for this world, whether the Indrori took my soul or not. There was no way out of the end game. No way to warn anyone else what the Indrori was up to after he took me down. I could only hope that Harper got herself out of Havenwood Falls before he had time to carry out his plan.

Wait. Maybe she could warn the others.

"Harper!" I shouted, knowing she wasn't here in the house, but praying she would hear me again. She did before, and I hadn't even been knowingly trying to reach her. "If you get this—get out of the town. Get everyone out! I can't stop it. The Indrori is going to take you all! Run!"

"It's too late, Tasha. Much, much too late."

His anger pulsed through all of their auras, causing the air around me to grow hot. It felt like I was at the gates of Hell. The cold of the spirit realm had become hotter than a sauna.

"Before we finish this, don't you know why we saved you for last? Why we didn't rip your soul out from your mother's womb thirty-two years ago when we first felt your presence?" the Indrori asked.

"Because that would have been impossible?" I spat.

"You underestimate our power!" the Indrori shouted as the spirits circled around me again and again. My head felt dizzy watching the skulls dance around me. "You humans always have," he went on. "What you fail to realize is that spirits know the *moment* their destroyer is made. It's a twist of cruel fate that we are not strong enough on our own to do anything about it. But together, as one united front, we've been able to stop any new Recoverers mere weeks after conception."

"What?" I gasped. That couldn't possibly mean what I thought it did.

"Oh, don't give me that look. Miscarriages happen all the time."

This thing really was evil. While I didn't care for kids myself, I would never want to harm them, let alone smother them completely.

"Why would you care about Recoverers?" I gasped. "We *help* humans stuck in the spirit realm! We save them from becoming lost between two planes for the rest of their existence. Why would you want to prevent us from that? I can see why you'd be pissed at us for trapping your ass, but why would helping save them from a life in purgatory tick you off?"

The Indrori pulsed with what I could only assume was anger.

"Did it never occur to you who might be pulling those lost souls to the other side in the first place? Souls stuck in purgatory are the easiest for us to manipulate. They require minimal energy to absorb. It's how we grew so strong so fast. Each one you rip away is another strike against us!" the Indrori raged.

I wasn't about to be intimidated. Not when I was already a goner. I would get my answers one way or the other.

"All right, fine, so why didn't you do the same to me? Why didn't you take me while I was still in the womb?" I shouted.

The swirling of the vortex slowed, but the grip on me didn't lessen.

"Because you, dear Tasha, are special. You have an aura that has been virtually impenetrable to us since your conception. Every time we've tried to take your soul, we have failed."

"How many times have you tried to kill me?" I heard myself ask.

"Three hundred and eighty-seven."

"Jesus," I whispered. That rattled me and gave me hope all at the same time.

"What makes you so confident you'll succeed this time, jackass?"

It probably wasn't smart to taunt this thing, but maybe this wasn't the end for me. Maybe I was stronger than they were?

"Why will we succeed this time?" the Indrori asked, forcing my attention back on the swirling spirits. "Because we finally figured out what the issue was. Your bloodline was too strong."

The Indrori's auras danced close to me again. Though they weren't physically touching me, I felt like I was being pinned down by a cement truck.

Just then, the Indrori's shape changed. A long branch broke away from the rest of the mass like a smoky tentacle.

"Sorry, this might hurt a little." The Indrori laughed.

Unable to move, I watched in horror as the tentacle slinked its way around my waist, mirroring the pattern of my snake tattoo. The smoke against my aura felt like a branding iron everywhere it touched. I let out a scream as intense pain enveloped my core. The tendril tightened around my spirit, and I heard a loud crack, followed by another. From the location of the pain, I knew it was breaking my ribs one by one. Because I was within two planes of existence, I could feel not only the heat of the aura's touch, but the physical pain of my human form crushing within its grip.

"I can destroy you now, Tasha, because I have absorbed your bloodline."

If I hadn't been in so much agony, I would have asked him what he meant, but as it stood, I was little more than a ragdoll. I couldn't see anything against the blinding white-hot pain. My thoughts were splintering, just like my spirit.

"You thought you could keep your parents safe from me, simply by cutting ties to them? Or maybe you just didn't know?" The Indrori waited for me to reply, but there was no way I could speak. I was in too much pain. I just wanted the pain to stop. *Please, make the pain stop.* "Foolish girl. Did it never occur to you that you inherited your dual ability from someone?"

I knew they were messing with my head now. My parents weren't like me. Far from it. My dad was a mailman, and my mom was a librarian. You couldn't find two more boring people on the planet. They didn't have the ability to bring back the dead. And they sure as hell never saw the spirits I did.

"It's rare, you know, to have a Seer and Recoverer marry, but to have both mutations passed down to their child? Unheard of. It's what set you apart, Tasha. That's what made you untouchable all these years. You had both of their DNA to protect you. We were most displeased."

I made a pathetic attempt to escape the vise grip I was in, but it made no difference.

"Think of it this way—at least you don't need to send them a Christmas card this year."

I shook my head violently, refusing to believe their words. My parents were fine. This was just a way to break down my spirit. Yet, at the same time, I knew the Indrori was telling the truth. It was the only thing that made sense, in a sick and twisted sort of way. My parents never really freaked out about my visions. They only told me to keep it secret. They never even took me to a doctor to get my head examined. Could they possibly have known what I was, because they had similar abilities?

"No!" I cried. A wave of anger shot through me, and the Indrori's grip suddenly lessened just enough so I felt a bit of relief.

"Interesting," the Indrori said. "You're stronger than we imagined. Even with the help of your parents' spirits inside of us, you are still proving to be a worthy foe."

The tendril squeezed around me one more time, and I knew it had just cracked another rib.

"Well, this is embarrassing. You seem to have drained us. Another soul to feast upon should do the trick, though. Perhaps someone strong and youthful, and good with a camera?"

Harper.

"No!" my raspy voice choked out, but it was too late. The Indrori had already dissipated through the floorboards, leaving me as emotionally drained as if I had been gutted like a deer.

The Indrori was taking away everything that mattered to me before it took my life. They were making me suffer the way they felt my kind had made them suffer. And there was absolutely nothing I could do about it.

CHAPTER 12

*A*lone in the house once again, I waited for a surge of energy to kick in. An adrenaline rush or something. This was my last opportunity to get out of here and try to save Harper and everyone else in Havenwood Falls, but I couldn't move. It felt like I was sitting in a pool of mud up to my neck. Their touch had drained me, much like I had drained them.

This was what Adam must have felt in his final moments. He, too, just sat there and let the Indrori take his soul. I understood now that it wasn't because he didn't want to fight the Indrori off, but because he literally couldn't. The hold that single tendril had on me was too strong. I couldn't imagine the pain of the Indrori's full form on me. I felt as though I was being burned alive. Even now, my skin was still hot where the tendril had coiled around me.

"Tasha!" A small but mighty voice pierced my mind. It was so faint, I thought I'd imagined it.

"Har-per?" My voice was thin. "Stay . . . away. Get . . . out." There was so much I wanted to say, but I didn't have the ability to do it.

"Save your voice. I heard your screams. I know you're hurt. I got your message loud and clear. I've been trying to get back into the house, but the Indrori is making it really hard. I might not be able to get back in just yet, but I can still help you from out here. The Court is rallying supernaturals.

Right now, we have to get you out of there. I tried to cage the Indrori on my own while it was attacking you, but I couldn't make him budge."

I tried to reply, to tell her that she needed to stay far away from here. She seemed to understand what I was about to say, because she answered my unspoken protest.

"Don't worry. I'm not anywhere near the house, but my ability—I can force demonic spirits to do my bidding, but this thing—it's too strong. The only way to save you is to get you out of there. But I need your help. How do you recover a soul? How do we bring you back to the human realm?"

If I had been able to laugh, I would have. The only way to recover my soul was with the help of another Recoverer. And the Indrori had wiped all of them out.

"Not possible. Save your . . . self," I gasped. Didn't she understand the danger she was in? That they all were in?

"Maybe Octavia can help?"

"Who?" I'd never heard of a Recoverer by that name, so it must have been one of her people, though it did sound vaguely familiar in some far away way.

"Octavia. She's a necromancer. She can bring back the dead. She's on probation, and she's not supposed to use her powers, but the Court could make an exception."

"No. Leave me. Save . . . self."

"I'm not leaving you to die! Roman will be there soon, Tasha. He'll know what to do. Stay with me."

I tried to shake my head even though she couldn't see the gesture. Roman wasn't going to help; he was the jackass that wanted me gone.

"Roman, traitor. In on it."

"You think Roman Bishop wanted you killed by this thing? He's an asshole, sure, but he's on the coven's High Council. He's been helping more than anyone to try to figure out a way to get you out. He went outside our original plan, because he has zero patience, but if he sent you in there alone, he had to have a reason."

As she spoke to me, the pain around my torso intensified. My flesh felt like it was burning. I cried out in pain. "Ah, God! Help me." I panted between waves of agony. "It's burning."

"Burning?" I heard Harper screech. *"Where is the fire? What is burning?"*

"Me. Skin. Burning. Everywhere. Harper. Hide. He's coming . . . you." I tried to focus my brain on getting Harper to safety, but the pain was too great. I tried to pinpoint what part of my body was hurting the most, but it really did feel like it was all over. My torso, my back, the base of my neck, even my Garden of Eden was burning. Wait. *The pain mirrored the exact location of my tattoo.*

What the hell?

I looked down at myself and noticed distinct orange glowing inside my aura. In fact, it looked like about ten scales of my tattoo along my midsection were glowing. Judging by the pain in other places, I was willing to bet there were glowing scales there, too.

"Harper," I croaked. "My tattoo . . . is glowing."

For several minutes there was no answer from Harper as I stared at the vibrant scales etched into my skin. Trying to focus on each spot of pain, I was guessing there were about twenty or so glowing patches spread around my body, but all within the confines of the tattoo. Was the Indrori branding me? Burning their dark energy into my flesh? Was this how it was going to end? In a blaze straight into Hell?

"Tasha," Harper said. *"Listen to me carefully. When did you get your tattoo?"*

When did I get my tattoo? What the hell did that have to do with anything? I was used to people asking about my ink because it was so unique, and because I had a knack for showing it off, but I couldn't see how knowing when I got it made any difference.

"It's probably nothing, but Roman is on the phone with me, and he's asking."

"Long time ago," I spat out between throbs of pain. Jesus, this hurt.

"Tasha . . . Roman said . . ." Her voice shook, which meant it couldn't be good news. *"He said* you *are the trap."*

I must have been losing my mind, because that statement made no sense. This was the end. It was likely a matter of minutes now before my brain turned into mush.

"Tasha, listen to me," Harper urged, trying to hold my attention, but it was waning by the second. I was so drained. *"Roman needs to know why you got your tattoo."*

These were probably my last moments left in this world, and Roman wanted to talk about my tattoo?

"To . . . cover gross . . . birthmarks," I said through gritted teeth. "More each year. Ah, fuck, this hurts!"

That's when I saw the telltale purple of the Indrori seep into the room. They were in the house, just below me now.

"Those weren't birthmarks, Tasha. Roman says they were ghosts you trapped. Wait, what?" I heard the confusion in Harper's voice as she relayed Roman's message to me.

"No. I used traps." I couldn't believe these were going to be my final words, an argument about the fundamentals of how I did my job.

"He said, 'Then why can no one else use the traps but you?' Tasha! You sent me in there knowing the trap wouldn't work for me?" she asked.

Whoops. Wait, I hadn't told her about the trap issue. Or Roman for that matter. Only my team members and Agent Duncan knew that. Roman must have bewitched Duncan or something to extract the information. Of course he did. Fucker.

"Tasha . . . those dark spots that showed up on your skin . . . Roman said they aren't all ink. The scales are the souls you've captured. They are trapped in your skin. You. Are. The. Trap."

As more and more purple smoke wafted into the room, I pondered what she said. Was it true? Is that why Adam could never figure out where the souls went from my traps? Was that why my skin felt like it was on fire now, because I had just absorbed some of the Indrori's demonic spirits?

I watched as the Indrori formed into one mass and couldn't help but notice that it didn't seem quite as large as it had moments ago. Maybe that was just my mind latching on to one last shred of hope.

Still, if I really was the trap, then this game was about to get interesting.

"You must be quite proud of yourself, Agent Young," the Indrori spat as he merged closer to me.

"Very," I said, my voice surprisingly strong now. If what Harper told me was true, this jackass was about to go down. If not, I was. Either way, this was going to end. Now.

"How did you warn the girl I was coming? I'm *dying* to know your secret."

"Guess that's just one of the many surprises there are about me that you will never know."

"Agent Young, there is nothing that I don't know about you. And once you are merged with me, there is nothing that will stand in our way. Not even your precious Collector."

I didn't know anything about a Collector, and right now I didn't care. All that mattered was how much I could egg this thing on and get it closer to me.

"You talk a big talk for a dead spirit floating."

The Indrori moved closer to me. Its form split again into a long tendril, and I suddenly realized I had no idea how to fight this thing.

"What do I do?" I shouted to Harper. In all the confusion and acceptance that I might be the weapon Roman said I was, I didn't actually think to ask *how* to use it.

"Tasha, he doesn't know. That's why he sent you in with the Indrori in the first place. He wanted to see your power in action. He wanted to know how you did it himself." I could hear the tears in her voice. *"I am so sorry. Look, I've left a message with Addie. She can help. I'm on my way with or without her. I'll be there as soon as I can."*

Great. I was to be a guinea pig for Roman's twisted sense of curiosity. Why didn't that surprise me? He was exactly the sort of guy who would throw me into a death pit to see how I'd manage. Jackass. And now Harper was on her way into this mess, and dragging another stranger in, too, but it would be too late.

"What do you do?" the Indrori asked, echoing the question I had posed to Harper. "You die, Agent Young. You die."

With that, the tendril coiled again around my aura, covering the faded blue of my aura with their own evil hue. All at once, I was paralyzed again. My soul was bending to their will. Crushing pain. Burning. Agony. I knew, even without looking, that I was glowing again. There was one difference, though. I wasn't scared anymore. This time, I understood the reason for the pain. Like I never had before.

In the past, whenever I took down a ghost, there was always a "kickback" from the trap—a heat that radiated off the gun. I realized now that it wasn't the gun. It was me. I was absorbing the aura's soul. Their energy was burned into my flesh. Just like Roman said. I was the trap. It hurt so much now simply because I was absorbing so many souls at once.

The longer the Indrori held me, the faster they would be caged. That knowledge sent a surge of energy through me. I didn't need to do anything but accept and receive their souls into my flesh.

"What . . . what are you doing?" the Indrori sputtered after a few minutes. They must have felt the shift in energy.

"Winning." I smiled.

The Indrori seemed to sense what I was doing, because he tried to release the tendril, but he couldn't. Unbeknownst to me, I had latched my own aura onto the Indrori. I was in control now.

Whatever I was doing simply by staying in contact with the Indrori was working, because his coloring was growing less intense by the minute. The sheer size was diminishing as well with each passing second. What used to fill up the entire bedroom now only commanded a fourth of it.

Now that I wasn't closing my eyes against the pain, I could see what was happening. Soul by soul, they were leaving the Indrori and filling the spots on my skin.

"Stop! Let me go!" a voice cried out that wasn't the Indrori, or at least, not the same voice I'd been accustomed to. This was one singular voice. An older woman, by the sound of it.

Her blue aura was screaming at me, and I realized her soul wasn't demonic, but there was nothing I could do to reverse what my body was doing on its own.

"What is happening?"

"Don't send me back!"

"Wait! No! Please!"

"Tasha!"

More pleas came, each time a different voice. Some were hostile, and some were confused, many of them victims in a game they wanted no part of. Some were evil through and through, judging by their color, but others—I could sense some were innocents. I felt conflicted about trapping them, but there was nothing I could do. Another force had taken over, and it wasn't going to stop until the job was done.

"Leave her alone!" a voice boomed. It was Harper. Beside her stood a massive lion. Like, a legit lion. With fucking wings on its back. The roar of it rattled the room.

"Meet Desi," Harper said.

Lion or not, neither of them was a match for this much energy.

"I . . . got this," I gasped. "Get out!" There was no way I could stop what I was doing to save Harper or her pet. I needed her to save herself. The Indrori seemed to swell against the challenge. It was too late. I could feel my grip weakening.

I screamed out to warn her as a bright flash of light filled my eyes. It turned the whole room white, and then there was nothing. Nothing left of the Indrori. Nothing left in the room. And most troublesome, nothing left of Harper. Unable to hold on to rational thought, I felt my eyelids close, and my body fall hard against the floor.

CHAPTER 13

*W*hen I awoke, it was to the sound of voices spoken in hushed tones. There was an odd buzzing in my ears, as though I'd just been through an explosion, or had been dropped on my head from a great height. Everything hurt.

"Hey, I think she's waking up." I felt a hand wrap around mine and knew without opening my eyes that it was Eduardo. I'd know the feel of those strong hands anywhere on my body. I felt my lips curl into a smile. The Indrori didn't kill him. It was a bluff. *Thank you, God.*

"Tasha?" I didn't recognize the female voice.

My eyes squinted open as the brightness of the sun blinded my senses. Jesus, it was bright in here. When I was able to focus, I looked down at Eduardo's hand in mine. I could *feel* his hand in mine. It was warm as it held me. His touch was warm. I was warm. And solid.

"How—how am I touching you?"

Eduardo smiled, but looked over to the girl sitting on the other side of me.

I turned to her, as though she could make sense of it all. Was I no longer in the spirit realm? Was I dead? Was this Heaven? It certainly was bright enough to be, though I would have thought Heaven would have come with a lot less pain. "Who are you? Where's Harper?"

"I'm Addie—Addie Beaumont. I came as soon as I got Harper's

message." She gave me a weak smile that didn't reach her eyes behind black-framed glasses. Like Harper, she wore an oversized hoodie and jeans. Unlike Harper, she had a piercing in her nose, and tattoos peeked between several bands of bracelets and where her sleeves rode up. Something about her made me like her instantly. "We were worried about you."

"Where is Harper?" I said again, this time slowly. I still didn't know who this woman was or why she was here or how I was even back in the human realm without the aid of a Recoverer.

"We were hoping you could tell us that?" a deep voice asked. Roman appeared beside Addie, and I tried to lunge for him. I instantly regretted it as pain shot through my rib cage.

"Easy, babe," Eduardo soothed. I let him push me back into the bed, not because I agreed that I needed to rein it in, but because I had no other choice. I was dizzy from the pain I'd just caused myself. The way my head was currently spinning, I would likely fall to the floor if I tried to stand up.

As I lay back, I noticed I had been changed into my normal clothes. Black slacks, black bra, and my white blouse. Eduardo must have helped me, because I didn't remember dressing myself. I didn't remember anything after latching myself onto the Indrori.

"What happened? Why am I so weak?" I croaked. Every muscle in my body felt swollen. No. That's the wrong way to describe it. I felt full. To the point of exploding out of my skin.

"Well, I'm guessing you have several broken ribs and extensive internal bruising, but I think your discomfort is a result of more than your physical injuries," Addie said.

Eduardo and I looked up at her, waiting for her to explain.

"I've been trying to communicate with some of the spirits trapped inside of you—" Addie began.

"Wait, you can hear them—inside my skin?" I looked down at my shirt and pushed it aside to look at my tattoo. Every single scale on my skin appeared to be filled in. "Holy shit," I whispered.

"Not in the same way Harper can. I'm a witch and a hellhound shifter, and since the spirits are denizens of Hell, I have other ways.

They're confused and angry—that's all I can discern. Judging by your color and weak pulse," she said, leaning in to check my complexion, "I'm going to guess that having this many souls trapped on you is not great for your health."

"Ya think? God, I feel like I need to be juiced, like that Violet kid in *Charlie and the Chocolate Factory*." My head was spinning from all this new information. Like what the hell a hellhound was.

Roman let out a huff. "That's it. She needs to go to the Infernum and release them," he said.

"Oh, now he cares about saving me," I said, flopping back onto the bed, feeling nauseous. "Seriously, guys. Where is Harper? She was there trying to fight off the Indrori one minute, there was a flash of light, then poof—both she and the Indrori were gone, and I somehow am back here feeling like a beached whale. What the fuck happened?"

"We have people working on Harper's whereabouts. Trust me, we are just as curious about where she went as you are. Right now, we need to worry about you."

I looked up and saw a woman walk into the room. She was an older lady, dressed in a dark business suit, her blond hair in a chignon.

"You found us," Roman said.

"Of course I did," the woman replied.

Roman huffed and turned his attention back to me.

"Look, Tasha, I know you're still pissed at me for tossing you in that house with no knowledge of what you were up against, but you were in no real danger. I had a handle on the situation. As planned, the hellhounds were on standby to bring you back if things got too bad, but I had to let you try. I had to know if you had the gift the Court believed you did." I glared at him. I didn't trust Roman in the slightest.

"Choose your words carefully, Roman. Just because we knew what she could do does *not* mean we condone the way you handled the situation."

Roman waved away her comment like an annoying fly.

"What if you had been wrong?" I asked.

Roman growled. Fucking growled. If I wasn't so out of it, I might have jumped him right then and there. It was hella hot. "If you failed," he said, "the Indrori would have been handled in other ways, but it wouldn't have worked for long." He came over to the bed. "Tasha, with the power they held, there would be no way to contain that much energy. Eventually, our tricks to hold them back would have failed. If your unique ability to separate an Indrori back into single souls again was real, we needed to know that. You were our last and only resort from that thing truly escaping the Infernum, if not today, then in the near future, especially if the Collector has anything to do with this."

Addie and the other woman both threw death glares at him. This Collector person kept coming up, but it was clear from their stares I wasn't about to pry any information out of them. Clearly, this was a town concern and sure as hell not mine.

"So why didn't you tell me that?" I said as vehemently as I could in my weakened state. "Why not be honest? Why not arm me with that information to protect myself?" My head spun just then, causing me to lose my balance, and my eyes rolled back in my head for a second.

"Tasha, you need your rest," Addie said, trying to get me to settle down. Eduardo had stood up, ready to punch out Roman if he so much as took a step closer to me.

I took comfort in that, even if Roman would likely flatten him if it came to blows. Eduardo was built, but Roman was a warlock, and he didn't play fair. Still, it was nice of Eduardo to stand guard for me, if only as a show of testosterone. He was trying to be the alpha. Silly puppy. He had no idea what he was up against.

"Telling you the truth would have slowed things down immensely. We're dealing with too many threats at once, so I took matters into my own hands with this particular one." He glanced at the woman beside him, who glared at him again. "Yes, yes, I know. We'll talk later, Saundra. Consider me properly hand-slapped," Roman drawled to the woman.

"This discussion is not over," she said. "For now, we need to get Tasha to the Infernum. I'll call the hellhounds. Addie, you can lead her there. The others will be waiting to help you."

Addie nodded, then Saundra left without allowing Roman another word.

"Addie is helping me, but who is helping Harper?" I asked, sitting up, though feeling like I was going to hurl. "Where did she go?"

Roman lowered his gaze, cutting off an answer he might have given me. Addie reached out a hand to me. It was hard to read her expression due to the tinted glasses she was wearing. "We have several of our people looking for her. I'm sure she's fine. Harper is still learning about her abilities. Her mace may have even pulled her out."

"Her what?"

"She has a mace—the weapon, not the pepper spray. It's a little like Thor's hammer. It can get her out of pickles. I'm guessing that's what happened, and she'll turn up soon enough. But for now, we really do need to get you taken care of." She reached out a hand as though to help me stand, which was the last thing I wanted to do.

"We should let her rest," Eduardo said, trying to push Addie away with just his glare.

"She can rest after she's shed those souls," Roman said. He walked over to the bed and took hold of my arm. "Let's go."

"Stay away from her!" Eduardo attempted, and failed, to swat his hand away. Roman looked at me for a moment, then adjusted his jacket and flared his nostrils ever so slightly. His left hand twitched. He'd better not pull any magic shit. I wouldn't stand for that. I needed to calm the situation down.

"Hey, babe?" I said, turning to Eduardo. "I'm so thirsty. Could you make me some tea or something? There should be a peppermint tea in the bags we brought." I tried to bat my eyes in the way that got me anything I wanted with him, but I was just too damn tired to pull it off.

"Of course." His eyes focused on me intently. "I'd do anything for you. You know that, right?"

My throat tightened at the emotion that suddenly got stuck there. I nodded once and watched him walk by Roman, his chest puffing as he did.

"Fine. After your tea, you'll shed." Roman walked over to the wingback chair in the corner, unbuttoned his jacket, and sat down in a way that indicated he was not happy with having to wait on me.

"Quick question," I said, closing my eyes against the bright sun for a moment. "Why do you keep saying I need to 'shed'?" I opened my eyes in time to see Roman glance at Addie, who exchanged an unspoken dialogue with him. They were holding something back. "Addie, what is he talking about?"

None of this was making any sense, but Addie was a friend of Harper, so I was hoping that meant she could be trusted to tell the truth.

"Fine. I'll tell her," Roman said with reluctance. His hand pressed against his lips in a tent formation as he seemed to consider his words. "There have been stories of someone else with your exact abilities. *One.* He died centuries ago, but he also 'wore' the souls of the dead on his skin. There are no pictures of him from that time, no printed records, only the stories passed down over the generations. They say he was marked in a similar way to you. He didn't have a tattoo so to speak, but he did have strange markings all over his body."

I sat up a little, suddenly very intrigued.

"The legends mention him only as The Lizard Man, because of the scale-like patches and his affinity for the desert. Twice a year, he would have to shed his gathered souls. He had no access to Hell or the Infernum—no reapers or hellhounds to help him—so the story goes that he went to the desert to release the souls as far away from civilization as possible. In all truth, The Lizard Man is an enigma." Roman clenched his jaw a few times. "We don't know if any of this is true or if it was just a ghost story people told to keep children from wandering into the desert."

Roman stretched his neck from side to side, showing off neck muscles exposed from where his shirt was undone at the collar. I resisted the urge to find that as sexy as it was.

He picked up the creepy-ass doll on the mantel and looked at it absent-mindedly before returning it back to its face-down position. "When I heard the rumors that another soul shedder was alive and in the United States, and working for the feds, no less, I had to find you."

"Soul shedder?" I raised an eyebrow, even though the term did sound kind of badass.

Roman didn't seem to hear my question, because he rattled on. "I had to see it with my own eyes. We were desperate, Tasha. The Indrori had breached their prison and for some reason, came here to Havenwood Falls. Our town didn't know how much danger it was in. We have other pressing issues—"

"Like this Collector dude?" I asked.

"Precisely. This Indrori business was the last thing we needed. There was no way to know that the Indrori was looking for you specifically."

"You should have stuck with the plan," Addie admonished, glaring at him. The way she stood up to him made me like her even more. I could see why Harper trusted her.

"When we found out you were a soul shedder, the Court was definitely intrigued. But their plan was cumbersome. Too many people involved. Too many ways for things to go wrong. Too much planning and ensuring everyone was safe."

"In other words, they had a sane approach to Tasha going up against an Indrori," Addie said, folding her arms in front of her chest.

Roman took a few steps toward her, but she didn't retreat. It was a power move for him, and one I was quite sure he got away with a lot. But not with her. He wouldn't have with me, either, if I were able to get out of this bed. Asshole.

"Back off," I hissed, hating that I was too tired to clock him over the head.

He turned his focus on me instead. "We didn't have time to waste, Tasha. They were too powerful. Who knows what damage they could have done to Havenwood Falls if I hadn't forced your skill?"

"So you didn't tell anyone that I was coming?" I stared him down, daring him to lie to me.

"I was planning on telling them. Eventually," Roman confessed.

I wanted to lay into him about how selfish it had been of him to risk my life and Harper's that way, but I found that I was too tired to fight with him. It really did seem as though I was carrying hundreds of souls on my skin. I could feel my flesh straining from the pressure of their auras. I was suddenly quite nervous. I wasn't sure how much longer I could hold onto all this energy.

"So what is the plan, then? I'm just supposed to go back to the Infernum—the place they escaped from, mind you—do the hokey-pokey, and all the souls come off me?"

Addie looked at me blankly, and I wondered if it was because of how insane I sounded, or if she was too young to know what I meant by hokey-pokey.

"I honestly don't know how you do it," Roman said. "How did you absorb them all?"

I thought back on it all. "I didn't do anything. I just sort of held on," I said.

Roman nodded as though that made complete sense. "I suppose then all you have to do to release them is to let go."

It sounded so easy and so impossible all at the same time.

CHAPTER 14

"*T*his will help with the nausea," Roman said, dropping a white powder in the tea when Eduardo brought it in.

"Hey, she's not drinking anything you poisoned, asshole. You've already drugged her once!" Eduardo shouted.

Eduardo wasn't wrong. He did get me to take those sleeping pills. Still, the way my stomach was lurching, I was willing to try anything. Even more sleeping pills. Anything to make the feeling subside.

"Give me the fucking tea or I'll hurl on your face," I said. Addie snickered at my side.

Eduardo looked between me and Roman before he sighed and relented.

After I sipped the tea that Eduardo made me, that I really didn't want, Addie told me that she was going to take me to a cemetery to gain access to the Infernum.

"Wait. Hold up. The entrance to the prison is in a cemetery?"

Addie shifted her glasses. "Yes, and the only way in is with me, so do not let me out of your sight."

"Says the lady who wants to take me for a stroll in the cemetery," I winced.

Roman grunted. "Hurry up and drink your damn tea. We need to leave."

"She'll take as long as she needs, buddy," Eduardo said.

In a flash, Roman snapped his fingers, and Eduardo's head fell onto his chest. Loud snores erupted from his lips as though he'd been asleep for hours. If I wasn't so pissed I'd actually be impressed with how fast the spell worked.

"What did you do to him?" I shouted.

"He's fine," Roman said in a bored tone. "He can't come with us. Humans aren't allowed in the Infernum. Addie can only take you. Let's go."

I glanced at Eduardo, who seemed quite content.

"Roman's right. He can't come. He'll be safe here," Addie assured me.

Just then a roll of nausea swept through me.

"Oh God." I held my hand to my mouth for a moment. "I thought this tea was supposed to help this?"

"It is," Roman hissed. "But even that won't hold long. We have to leave. Now."

I suddenly didn't want to test Roman's theories about how much worse I might feel if I didn't shed these souls. I swung my feet out and tried to stand, but I had a hard time supporting all the energy on me.

"Grab her arm," Roman ordered Addie. "If anyone looks at us, she's drunk. We're taking her home to sleep it off. Got it?"

Addie nodded. Secrets had to be kept, after all. Even if I was carrying over a hundred souls on my flesh, to the outside world, I was reduced to a lush. How lovely.

A few seconds later, we were in a car, driving. I wasn't sure how long we drove before we stopped, and they pulled me out. I kept fading in and out of alertness. The tea was definitely wearing off, and the waves of pain were getting more intense by the step.

"Where the hell are we going? I don't know how much longer I can take this," I gasped as they dragged me down a cement walkway. My head bobbed up and down as we went through the cemetery. I was trying really hard not to pass out, but this constant jostling around made that difficult. Everything went dark for a moment, like we were going through a tunnel, or maybe I blacked out. I couldn't tell if what I was seeing was real or if I was hallucinating.

Roman shifted my weight. "It's right up ahead. I can't go any farther. Addie, can you handle her?"

I didn't see her answer, but I felt her taking my weight fully against her side.

"Liam and Savage are waiting for you . . . below," Roman said to Addie.

If she replied, I didn't hear. I just felt my body being dragged along the grass past graves that danced in the moonlight. We stopped in front of what looked like a mausoleum.

"What's happening?" I said, trying my best to hold onto focus.

"Okay, Tasha, Liam and Savage are hellhound shifters. They'll take us into the Infernum. Whether they're in their human forms or in their hellhound forms, you can*not* look into their eyes. Understood?'

"Why not?"

"Oh, no biggie, really. It's just that their stares could kill you if you do."

"Commencing eye closing," I said, snapping my eyes shut.

"Hang onto me, and don't open your eyes. You're going to feel like you're falling, which you are, but trust me, you won't be hurt so long as you keep your eyes closed and hang onto me. Got it?"

"Hold on. Eyes Closed. Copy that. If you were a guy and you had a blindfold, this might actually be kinda kinky." I tried to laugh, but my stomach rolled. "Let's just get there," I groaned.

Addie's arm wrapped tight around my waist, and I closed my eyes. That's when we took a step off what I could only envision as a cliff. It took everything in my power not to open my eyes against the sensation of falling. I swear, we fell for miles. I couldn't even begin to imagine what could be this deep.

"Almost there. Hold on," Addie said over the wind.

And then, all at once, we weren't moving.

"You can open your eyes."

I took a moment to catch my breath before I risked a look. There was very little to see. Darkness surrounded everything. In the distance were hulking figures coming toward us. They carried with them the only light I could see. Bright yellow light seemed to radiate off their bodies. From this distance, they looked like wolves on steroids. It was the sound, though, that did me in. It brought me to my knees. Screams. Thousands of screams coming from every direction. I couldn't tell if it was coming from the darkness or from the souls trapped inside me.

"Okay, time to close again. The hounds are coming."

I did as instructed, mostly because I needed to escape from the reality I was in. I just wanted the pain to stop. For the screaming to stop. For the darkness to finally be lifted.

"We're inside the Infernum. The hellhounds will help trap the souls you shed. So just do your thing. We'll take it from here."

I wanted to ask more questions. I wanted to know the specifics of how it would all go down, but without warning, a wave of pain came over me. All my muscles constricted. I heard myself scream, but in a voice that wasn't my own.

"Tasha?" Addie said. I felt myself curl into a tight ball.

"Stay back," I whispered in warning.

"Let go, Tasha. It's safe here." I wasn't sure if Addie said that, or even if I had uttered the words myself. All I knew was that the phrase felt like the turning of a faucet. This was a safe place. I wouldn't hurt anybody. I didn't need to hold on anymore.

Laying on the ground, I clutched at my stomach. It felt like the worst menstrual cramps of my life, but spread out over every scale on my skin. The pain was worse than when I'd absorbed them. Jesus Christ! I hadn't anticipated shedding to be this painful. Then again, I was about to birth some pretty pissed off souls.

A scream tore through me as I opened my eyes and watched the first soul leave my skin. It emerged wisp-like, from the fabric of my waist band. It glowed red, and I could hear the voice of the aura shouting in time with my own cries. Before the spirit could travel far, there was a golden flash of light, and the sound of growls as a hellhound bounded after the released spirit. I didn't have time to consider the mechanics of how any of this worked, because a scream from both myself and the aura began anew.

On and on this went. Pain, hellhound, repeat. I heard the screams of each soul that came out of me. Several cursed my name and vowed to find me, but I knew they were empty threats. Even if they got out and did find me, I'd trap them again. There was some comfort in that.

"Tasha?" It was a voice I recognized.

Adam's voice pierced through the pain. I opened my eyes and saw his aura floating out of my side. The panic in his voice rattled my bones.

"Adam!" I reached out to try to grab him, but his aura was already being pulled away by a hound.

"No! That's my partner. Stop!" Another wave pulled through me, causing all thought of Adam to leave my mind. Blinding pain radiated from above my chest as another soul was close on his heels. How much more of this could I physically endure? I felt like I was going to split in two. One shed merged to the next until it just became nothing but agony.

The one voice I expected to be the loudest, however, never came. The Indrori's voice was silent. That voice was the amalgamation of souls that spoke for the whole. Once I separated them, their control was no more.

When the last soul had been shed, I could tell. My body felt like my own again, though very, very tired. I closed my eyes. I needed to sleep, for like a thousand years. This cold, dirty ground would do just fine.

CHAPTER 15

hen I woke up, it was to a strange room. I expected to awaken in a hospital, or the morgue, truth be told. Definitely not in a cozy-looking bedroom. Sitting beside me, with her back ramrod straight in a chair near the door, was the woman Roman had called Saundra.

"Ah, she's awake at last," she said as I pushed myself up into a sitting position. I expected to feel groggy or in pain, as I had been prior to my shedding, but to my surprise, I felt quite agile and full of energy. Even my ribs felt better. "We haven't been properly introduced. I'm Saundra Beaumont. I sit on the Court of the Sun and the Moon and the High Council of the Luna Coven. I'm sorry to have met you the way I did. I want to extend my sincere apologies for the unfortunate way you have been treated. However, we are here to help and protect you now. As we should have done from the moment you arrived."

"Where am I? Why don't I hurt?"

"You're at Whisper Falls Inn." She shifted in her seat. "I had Dr. Underwood tend to your injuries."

I didn't know who Dr. Underwood was, but I had to assume he was a supernatural if Saundra called on him. I was no expert, but I knew cracked ribs weren't something that healed overnight, so magic must have been in play.

Glancing around the room, I noticed that, while the room was homey, there were no giant stuffed animals or flowers laid out, which meant Eduardo hadn't been here yet. He liked to spoil me whenever he got the chance.

"Guess Eduardo and Harper haven't been here yet?" I asked.

Something in Saundra's eyes flickered. "No one knows your location but me and Michaela, the inn's owner."

My eyebrows shot up, instantly questioning her motives for keeping me hidden away. I didn't know her at all and had no idea if she was good or evil, truth be told. She seemed to follow my train of thought, because she put up her hands briefly in surrender. "It's only so that you could recover in your own time without a million people hovering over you. You needed peace and quiet, so I saw to that."

I relaxed a little. "Well, thank you for that, I guess. How long was I out?"

"Three days."

At that, I bolted upright. "Three *days*?" That's when I noticed the IV attached to my arm.

"I'm surprised it was only that long," Saundra said flippantly. "I would have expected at least a week after your ordeal, but then again, you are a bit of a mystery."

It was hard to believe I'd been asleep that long, but after what I'd endured, I was surprised I wasn't dead.

"Eduardo," I said, knowing he was probably worried about how I was doing, too. "I need to see him." He was probably tearing up the town, trying to find out where they had taken me.

"I'm afraid that will be quite impossible."

"And why is that?" I asked, not enjoying the finality of her tone.

"The Court met, and it was decided it was best that Eduardo's memories of Havenwood Falls—and of you—be wiped clean."

"Wiped clean? What the hell are you talking about?"

She placed her hands on her lap in a slow and methodical way.

"It means just what you think it means. And before you think about it, even if you were to find him, which you won't, he wouldn't remember you, or anything about his time in Havenwood Falls."

I stared at her for a few moments, waiting for her to tell me that she was joking or that I'd misheard her, but it became clear that she had really sent him away. She'd erased him from my life.

"Who said you could do that? You don't have the right to—"

"Actually, I do, Agent Young. This is *our* town you're in. We have full say who stays and who goes."

My nostrils flared in anger.

"And my partner was a threat to your stupid little town?"

Saundra's upper lip twitched at the insult, but she kept her composure. "Your human 'friend' was never a threat among a town of supernatural beings, Tasha. He was, however, a threat to you."

She wasn't making any sense. Eduardo wouldn't hurt me. Not possible.

"Please, enlighten me," I snapped.

Saundra pursed her lips, seemingly annoyed that she had to explain her rationale to the dumb human. "Do you love him?" she asked.

"He's my partner."

She frowned. "Yes, I know. That wasn't an answer, though."

"I fail to see how my being in love or not with him has anything to do with why you sent him away!"

"It has everything to do with it."

I opened my mouth to ream her out for daring to assume how I felt. How dare she say I didn't love him. She didn't know anything about me or our relationship. But I couldn't articulate a proper argument. I cared for him, had fun with him, and we fit together perfectly, but I would never love him. I was just too wild to be tied down. At least, not yet. I knew he was falling for me, and I had done nothing to discourage him. It had been cruel of me to lead him on. Truth was, I held on to him so close because he was the only person I had whom I had ever considered a friend. It was selfish of me to hold on to him when my ultimate goal was going to be to let him go. Saundra had done him a kindness by erasing me from his memory.

"No, I didn't love him," I admitted at last. "I'm not capable of loving anyone but myself."

Saundra nodded. "That is precisely why I sent him away. He had fallen for you in ways that human men fall for beautiful women. But you are not normal, Tasha. You never have been. You're gifted, even among the supernatural. Your ability to absorb souls won't go away. There will always be lurkers within your flesh. You will always be tied to the spirit realm. You can't expect a human to be able to deal with such a burden."

As much as I hated to hear it, she was right. I wasn't normal. Why did I think I'd ever be able to have a normal relationship with a guy?

"Besides," she went on, "a puppy-dog crush would get in the way of the work we need you to do here in Havenwood Falls."

I couldn't help it. I laughed straight in her face. "You want me to work for *you*? After the shit your town pulled on me? Dragging me here without telling me the truth, allowing one of my best agents to be killed, imprisoning his aura, and then sending away a guy I was seeing?"

Saundra sighed. "What happened to your partner, Adam, was unfortunate. However, we were able to retrieve his aura during your shed. He has been released into our custody and supervision within Havenwood Falls."

"Wait? Adam is alive?" I asked, not daring to believe it.

Saundra shook her head. "No. Not in the way you're thinking. Too much time had passed for that. His vitals were weak back at the house. He was brain dead, as I'm sure you knew. The only way to salvage the best part of him was to allow him to cross over. We provided him with the option to stay here or to wander the earth. He chose to stay."

Adam's aura was intact. His soul had been saved. My eyes overflowed with emotion. I'd be able to see him again, even if he was only a spirit now.

"Can I see him?"

She nodded. "Soon. He's here, actually. In the inn with Madame Luiza, another spirit. She's giving him the tour."

"I wonder what color his aura is now?" I whispered to myself.

"Color?" Saundra asked.

I shook my head. "Nothing. I see an aura's color. It matches the mood they are in. He was blue the last time I saw him. Confused."

Saundra seemed bewildered by this. "Oh, well, I'm sure you'll find Adam looks very different now that he is no longer confused. He's a striking man. It's no wonder Madame Luiza is monopolizing him. She's a wicked flirt."

"Wait. You can *see* Adam?"

"Of course. He's more translucent then he was when he was alive, but his features are still quite present."

I stared at her for several minutes. Was this what happened to a spirit when they got to choose their fate? Was I only able to see auras in a state of distress? Or could she see ghosts differently than I could? There was so much to process.

"We're quite pleased he has chosen to stay. He will make an excellent addition to Havenwood Falls. I'm hoping you'll choose to do the same, Tasha. We could use your abilities here," Saundra said.

Pulling my emotions back in check, I turned my attention to Saundra.

"I hate to inform you, lady, but I already have a job. One that pays quite well. I get to travel on someone else's dime and rid the world of asshole souls at the same time. Why do you think I'd want to stick around a dump like this?" I asked, ticked at her audacity, thinking I'd actually stay here after everything that happened.

Saundra stood up and walked over to the window and pulled back the drapes. The sun had gone down, but I could see the streetlamps and Christmas lights twinkling in the darkness. "Because I know what you want, Tasha. What you really long for, more than anything else. It's something money and a million air miles could never grant you, but we can."

"Oh, really? What's that?"

She turned around and clasped her hands in front of her again. "A place to call home."

I stared at her blankly, unable to articulate my response. How the hell could she know that's what I longed for, when I'd never mentioned it to another living soul? I wondered, suddenly, if she could read my thoughts.

"Think it over," she said, before she crossed through the room and left me alone.

Damn it all. She was right. I had been searching for years for a place where I fit in, where I was accepted for my oddities. Now that I'd discovered my true identity as a soul shedder, I was going to have a ton of questions. Questions only a town like this had any hope of providing answers for.

For several moments I sat in silence, trying to process everything that happened. Just when I was ready to get out of bed and hunt her down to ask my questions, there was a knock on the door. The person on the other side didn't wait for an answer before they opened the door.

Addie walked in, wearing a black hoodie with a pentagram on it, jeans, and knee-high leather boots.

"Hey, how you feeling?" Addie asked, shutting the door behind her.

"About a hundred souls lighter. You?"

"I'm feeling a lot safer now that those spirits are back where they belong. Thank you, Tasha. That could have gotten really ugly."

I laughed. "I don't know, it was pretty rough from where I was lying."

"Right. Sorry."

I shook my head. "It's okay. Hey, did you find Harper yet?"

Addie's expression shifted, her gaze dropping. "No. We haven't given up, but . . . she's just gone. We can't find any trace of her. Her mace, Desi, has been hunting for her nonstop. It's like she disappeared off the face of the planet."

"Was she pulled into the spirit realm?" If she had been taken by the Indrori before I took it down, then maybe she was just between planes. I could recover her. "If she's in the spirit world, I could—" That's when it struck me how many days I'd been asleep. Too much time had passed. I wouldn't be able to recover her.

"I don't think she's passed on," Addie said, stopping my train of thought.

"Well, what happened to her then?"

Addie took a breath, as though debating how much to tell me.

"Please. She . . . she helped me when no one else would. If I can help you figure out where she is, I have to try," I plead.

"I shouldn't be telling you this. You aren't even a ward of the town."

"But I was with her when she disappeared. Maybe there is a piece to this puzzle I can help with," I argued. I wasn't just going to give up on Harper. She didn't give up on me. Even when her life was on the line.

"The Court thinks that the Indrori and the Collector may have been working together."

"You keep mentioning the Collector. Who is he?"

Addie stood up and walked over to the window. She seemed to gaze outside for the longest time before she spoke. "We don't know much, really. Someone who calls themselves the Collector has been threatening people in our town. Including Harper. The fact that Harper showed up in this house with the Indrori makes us think that they were working together to take Harper down."

"Wait, so you think Harper was the target?" I shook my head vehemently. "No. The Indrori clearly wanted me dead. They told me point blank their plans to destroy me."

"I know. Which is why I think the Court may be wrong on this. I don't think they were working together. I think the Collector saw an opportunity to take Harper and used the distraction of the Indrori to his advantage."

"It would be the perfect setup. But how would the Collector even know Harper was there?"

Addie turned around. "There is a lot the Collector knows that we can't figure out." She lifted her hand and tugged absently on her shirt.

"What aren't you telling me?" Nervous twitches were a dead giveaway when a person was trying to be secretive.

"It might be nothing . . ."

"Tell me."

Addie came back to the chair and sat down. She bit her lip for a moment before she spoke.

"When we were in the Infernum, Liam, one of the hellhounds you saw, said when returning some of the souls you shed to their prison, some of them . . . their signatures smelled different when he returned them to that section of the Infernum. He couldn't pinpoint what was off about it, but it was different than any of the other souls he'd dealt with. It might be nothing."

"Or it could be everything," I said.

"How so?" Addie asked.

"I don't know. It's just . . . Harper said something like that, too. That her powers—they were working differently with me. She said it was like everything was backward somehow."

Addie shrugged. "Harper's gifts are still emerging, though. That might just be her growing into new gifts. I'm sure we'll figure it out. We just have to keep thinking."

"I could help," I heard myself say. "I could go back to the house. See if her spirit is there . . . I mean, maybe she's trapped. I wouldn't be able to bring her back, but I might be able to find her, at least."

Addie smiled, then patted her black bag. "If you're sticking around, you're gonna need one of these."

"One of what?" I glanced at the bag.

Addie rolled her eyes. "Saundra didn't explain what I do, did she?"

"Besides saving my ass? No."

That prompted a laugh. "When I'm not out being a badass hellhound, a witch, and saving your ass, I'm also the town's resident tattoo artist."

I should have guessed she was a witch. That's why she and Roman seemed to have a shorthand I couldn't pick up on.

"Oh. Do you work at Tragic Ink?" I asked, remembering the shop Davis at Coffee Haven had told me about. Her working there would be cool, but I wasn't sure why she was bringing it up now.

"Nope. I work for the Court. I'm the business manager and responsible for the Registry."

She sat down beside me, placed a black leather bag on my bed, and took out several tattooing instruments.

"Um, are you giving me a tattoo?" I asked.

"Yep. That's why I'm here. Saundra really didn't tell you anything about this?" She sighed as though she was used to having to do the dirty work. "It's my job to mark the residents and visitors of Havenwood Falls. It's how the Court keeps tabs on the supernaturals. Makes sure we're not breaking any rules, stuff like that."

"Yeah, Roman Bishop told me a little about it. They act like an ankle monitor, right?"

"Yes and no." She dug into her bag again.

"Does it zap us if we get out of line?"

She stopped rifling in her bag to look at me. "Of course not. That's not how we are. It only works with the wards on the town. If there's trouble, the Registry gives us an idea of who we need to track down for the cause of it. See, I infuse the ink with magic that connects with the energy of the wards, so we know who comes and goes. But we only care if there's a problem. Otherwise, we don't pay any attention. And the magic also gives everyone a benefit. So it's a mark of freedom, in a way. It's a symbol that we belong. That we are a community."

I hadn't thought of it that way. When she said it like that, it seemed like the tattoos were a badge of honor. Something to wear with pride, not shame. I sort of liked the sound of that.

"Although, you've got a killer tat already," Addie said nodding toward my torso. Smiling, I reached down, lifted my shirt, and showed her the snake coiled around my body. The scales were no longer filled in.

"Woah," we both said at the same time.

"They're all gone," I whispered, running my fingers over the thin black outline of the scales. I really had shed them. "These were all black before," I said in wonder. "I wear demonic spirits, apparently. Until I get full, and then, I shed—like a snake—and off to the Infernum they go."

"You have a wicked gift." Addie didn't even bat an eye at how bizarre the statement was. Instead, she seemed . . . impressed.

"Yeah, it's kind of wild." I laughed, realizing how comfortable I felt chatting with Addie.

"A snake is such a fitting tattoo, given your abilities," she said, admiring the handy work.

"It is?" I would never in a million years attach spirits to snakes.

"Well, sure," she said, pulling on a pair of gloves. "I mean, a snake has long been used in medical logos, for good reason."

I paused to remember the snake and staff images on my own medicines in the past. Why *did* we use a snake logo for medicine? I'd never stopped to think about it. Addie seemed to realize I was clueless, because she gave me a small smile and went on.

"Greek mythology has long believed that snakes are sacred beings. Their venom was used for healing rituals and such, but their skin—the shedding of their flesh—that was a symbol of renewal and rebirth. Just like a life cycle. We live, we die, we are reborn as spirits. It's also kind of like you right now. You get a chance to reinvent yourself here, in Havenwood Falls."

I didn't answer her as my fingers traced over the outline of my tattoo. I eyed her bag with interest. She must have seen my eyes wander, because she brought the bag closer.

"You can pick any design you want," she said, "and you can choose anywhere you want it. I can make it visible or invisible, that's your call. The only question I need to know before we start is, am I making you a visitor tattoo or a resident one?"

I stared at her for the longest time, hoping she would pick for me. Did I want to go home, well, back to living in hotels and dating strings of men who would never fill the void in my heart, hiding away my gifts from anyone outside the FBI? Or did I want to give this rinky-dink town a shot, with their promise of accepting me for the freak show that I was? Did I want to shed the old me and step into in a new place? A place that held the promise of home . . .

Addie looked up at me with expectant eyes, and I smiled.

"Resident."

We hope you enjoyed this story in the Havenwood Falls series featuring a variety of supernatural creatures. Wondering what happened to Harper? Read *The Collector: Awakening.* Sneak peek an excerpt at the end of this book.

Havenwood Falls is a collaborative effort by multiple authors. Other books you might enjoy in the main Havenwood Falls series:

Ink & Fire by R.K. Ryals
From the Embers by Amy Miles
How the Dead Lie by Stacey Rourke

Also look for the YA line, Havenwood Falls High; the historical paranormal line, Legends of Havenwood Falls; the sexier side of town, Havenwood Falls Sin & Silk; the local supernatural college, Sun & Moon Academy; and the Havenwood Falls holiday short story anthologies.

Stay up to date at www.HavenwoodFalls.com

ABOUT THE AUTHOR

Danielle Bannister lives with her two children in Midcoast Maine, along with her precious coffee pot and peppermint mocha creamer. She is a writer of all things swoon-worthy, angsty, and snarky. She holds a BA in Theatre from the University of Southern Maine and her master's degree in Literary Education from the University of Orono. Her writing includes a collection of short stories called *Short Shorts*; The Twin Flames Trilogy: *Pulled*, *Pulled Back*, and *Pulled Back Again*; *The ABC's of Dee*; *Enigma*; *Doppelganger*; *Must Love Coffee*; and *Netherworld* and *Hollow Earth* with co-author Amy Miles.

ACKNOWLEDGMENTS

I want to thank Kristie Cook, R.K. Ryals, Randi Cooley Wilson, and E.J. Fechenda for letting me play with their characters and locations. I offer my apologies to them for the million and one questions I asked them in order to make sure I was getting their ideas correct. It is challenging to write in a world where so much has already been established, but these ladies helped me immensely until my romance brain slowly learned how the fantasy world worked. I am ever humbled.

AN EXCERPT

~ A Havenwood Falls New Adult Novel ~

HAVENWOOD FALLS

THE COLLECTOR: AWAKENING

KRISTIE COOK

R.K. RYALS BELINDA BORING

NADIRAH FOXX

The Collector: Awakening (A Havenwood Falls Novel) by Kristie Cook, R.K. Ryals, Belinda Boring & Nadirah Foxx

A witch, an angel, and a psychic face off with a supernatural force terrorizing their hometown—with its eyes set on the world.

Addie Beaumont, witch and future coven leader, loves her hometown of Havenwood Falls and would do anything to protect it. So when the supernatural village is threatened by a mysterious entity only known as the Collector, she's the natural choice to lead a task force to identify and stop him.

With little information about the Collector, Addie recruits psychic Harper Sinclair, who channels demons, and angel Micah Westbrook, protector of a teenaged oracle. But Harper's messages from Hell reveal only doom and gloom, and Micah refuses to contact the Divine, which could invite something much more dangerous to town.

But then people are attacked. Harper vanishes. And Micah's young ward is targeted next.

Micah must learn to trust Addie and this town to help protect his charge. Harper must embrace the darkness within her and control the demons before they control her. And Addie must face the fact that not everyone will go as far as she will to defend their home. But if she and the others fail in battle, the Collector will not only overtake Havenwood Falls, but will move on to the rest of the world. For this enigmatic entity has only just awakened.

THE COLLECTOR: AWAKENING

PROLOGUE

Wind whipping at her hair and cloak, Camellia carefully climbed the snow-dusted, rough-hewn stone steps up the side of Mount Mae, in the southeast corner of the box canyon known as Havenwood Falls. The town spread out far below, the buildings' roofs no more than tiny squares and rectangles still noticeable among the budding trees. In another month or so, many of those roofs would be camouflaged by greenery. Camellia couldn't really see much, however, because she was in the clouds. Quite literally. Way up here, above the tree line and near the top of one of the highest peaks in the state of Colorado, the snow swirled thickly around her, and the small village below seemed to belong to a different world.

She paused to glance around, peering into the near white-out for the monolithic-like stone that marked her destination. Pinpointing it slightly ahead and to her right, she realized she had almost passed by it and likely would have wandered in circles in what were quickly becoming blizzard-like conditions. For the Collector's estate would have never shown itself if she hadn't found that stone. Bracing herself against the wind once more, she tightened her hand around her cloak, pulling it close, and pushed her way upward to the landmark. As soon as her palm pressed on it, magical energy coursed through her, and the cloud of snow cleared, revealing a large estate. The structure—all glass, wood beams, and stone—seemed to crawl up and into the stony peak as though a natural part of it.

A dark, cloaked shape stood at the top of the steps, in front of the massive wooden door. Seeing that Camellia had arrived, the figure stepped backward, disappearing through the entryway. Camellia followed, hurrying into the warmth of the mansion. Although all of the glass should have let in plenty of natural light, she plunged into darkness upon entering. She was expecting it, though. The Collector was not exactly forthcoming with his—or her or its—identity. Camellia only knew what she *needed* to know—that this entity was one powerful son of a bitch. She hadn't lived as long as she had by being stupid, so she never questioned, never protested, never demanded to know more. She obeyed, and she was rewarded for it. Handsomely.

Movement ahead led her into a large dark room furnished with several seating areas. Camellia hurried to the one near the fire on the far wall. The firelight barely reached the nearest chair, but its warmth beckoned her. She sensed more than saw the Collector take a seat in a high-backed chair angled just right so she could see nothing more than the cloaked shape.

Although she couldn't see the Collector's face, she could feel the intense gaze on her, appreciating her new form. New compared to the last time they met, anyway. "You look exactly like her."

"You sound surprised. This is what you wanted, yes?"

The head bobbed once. "Yes, of course. What news do you have for me about our beloved little town?"

Camellia wasn't sure, but she thought she heard a hint of sarcasm drop on the word *beloved*. She certainly held no sentiments for the town of Havenwood Falls, but she hadn't quite been able to discern the Collector's true feelings for it. The Collector was a complete enigma, one whose secrets would only be revealed by peeling back layer after layer—and she had a feeling there were thousands of layers. She may never know much about this entity before her. Although intrigued, she wasn't sure if she really cared to. She knew the Collector was a powerful being, more powerful than anything else in this canyon, which was saying a lot. She was certain she didn't want to be around when that power was finally unleashed.

"News," the Collector repeated, more a demand now than a question.

Camellia cleared her throat before announcing, "Michaela Petran is indeed back in Havenwood Falls. The inn's ownership has been transferred to her."

"Excellent. And the curse on her and the Roca bloodlines?"

"The Luna Coven has contained it to the eldest Roca boy, just as you expected they would do."

"Excellent, excellent." Quiet appreciation could be heard in the Collector's voice, deep and raspy with both feminine and masculine properties, making it impossible to discern the Collector's gender simply from aural cues. "If he doesn't cooperate, we can use that in our favor. We'll help him turn strigoi, and the Court will eliminate him for us."

"I think he will cooperate, though. He seems to feel remorse for his actions."

The Collector nodded, long fingers tapping against the chair's arm. "Good, good. Then our plan should work, especially with Adelaide's assistance. She has a soft spot for both the Petrans and the Rocas. She'll encourage him to do the right thing—support the Petrans and help restore the inn to the glorious place it once was. And while they're at it, we need him to find the Eye of Valerian. The magic it holds . . ."

The voice drifted off with a sound of reverence, making Camellia wonder just how much magic the artifact held for the Collector to want it so badly. Or perhaps quantity wasn't the point. Maybe it was the type of magic that was coveted—the dark type.

"May I offer him a bonus for it?" she asked.

"Of course." The Collector tsked. "These people and their money . . . They have no idea what's truly valuable. Speaking of, do you have the list?"

Camellia fished in her cloak's pocket and pulled out her phone. "Yes, here."

"You broke into the Tomb under the Academy?" The Collector sounded mildly impressed. Sun and Moon Academy was magically warded, and only those in the Order of Castor, a secret society, knew about the Tomb below the library.

"You hired me for my shape-shifting abilities. It's not difficult to sneak in when you look exactly like someone who belongs there."

"I suppose so." The Collector muttered something about troubles and Loki. A leather-gloved hand flipped out of the shadows. "Let me see what the Court thinks they're hiding from me."

Camellia flipped through the images on the phone, then handed it over. "This is a list of all the artifacts in their possession, and if you slide to the next picture, another list, of those they seek."

The Collector gazed at the screen, perusing the first image. "I know exactly where the Blue Dragon Dagger is. It is safe where it's being hidden—for now. The Lantern of Tír na nÓg would be useful, and now that Akeel has passed, it should be easier to attain. We'll work on that later. Many of these are not what they think they are, and I know there are others in that town and surrounding it that they undervalue." With a swipe of the finger, the screen changed. "Ah! There it is. The Elan Chain. They apparently don't know there is already at least one link in the canyon. I believe more are headed this way, if they hire that Egyptian woman as the high school history teacher. We need those links. They are of utmost importance. Even more than the Eye of Valerian. If Hermod finds them . . . I *will* not let him win again!" The Collector banged a bony fist on the arm of the chair.

"I'm sorry—who?" Camellia asked, bemused.

"Nothing," the Collector growled quietly. "My concern. Not yours."

Camellia dipped her chin. "I'll see what I can find out about the Elan Chain."

The Collector gave a dismissive wave. "No, not your concern, either. I have other sources. I need you to keep your focus on obtaining the moroi artifact. I also need you to reach out to Rachelle. With what's coming . . . I need her as my eyes and ears again. It's time she returns to Havenwood Falls and infiltrates the town. She did well in gathering intelligence last time. She did so much for us then, and I have a sneaking suspicion she'll be happy to resume her efforts. Her feelings toward the town and its people are not exactly warm."

"Do I keep this appearance?" Camellia currently wore the skin of Magda, a witch and a member of the town's precious Luna Coven. A former member, anyway. Now she was wanted. "The Court searches for her."

"Not in town, then. You will have to arrange to meet with Mr. Roca outside of town. He's familiar with that appearance, comfortable with it. He'll be more apt to trust Magda and cooperate. Otherwise, when you're in town, be someone new. Unassuming. A frumpy, middle-aged man or something."

Camellia nodded. "I know just the shape."

"Then you know what must be done. And Camellia? You understand the consequences of exposing me." It was not a question, but a reminder.

Camellia averted her gaze, ducking her face in a near bow. "Completely."

"Go on, then. Find Rachelle. And bring me the Eye of Valerian. Your stipend has already been added to your account."

Camellia dipped her head once more, hiding the small smirk on her lips. She'd continue working for the Collector for as long as it proved beneficial—and the money waiting in her account was very beneficial. But when that was no longer the case, she'd just been armed with a wealth of information, and she knew full well that information was power.

Which was exactly why she hadn't disclosed everything she knew to the Collector.

~

CHAPTER 1 ~ ADDIE

The wind howled through the box canyon, blowing snow sideways, the sharp edges of its frozen teeth slicing through my parka and biting into my skin. I usually wasn't bothered much by the cold. Up until a few months ago, I'd chalked it up to the fact that I'd grown up in this small town in the Colorado Rockies, where winter was a way of life. Now I knew there was another reason my body stayed warmer than others'. Something I didn't want to think about now—or ever. I was a witch, damn it, and highly trained and naturally powerful at that. Nothing else mattered.

I pulled my coat tighter against me, not even bothering to spell myself against the cold—it'd be a witchy thing to do, but I was glad to feel the chill of one of our coldest nights yet this winter. It meant I *was* more witch and less . . . other. The thing I didn't want to think about.

Peering through the blowing snow, I eyed the looming shape of City Hall, a dark shadow on the far side of Town Square Park. I'd had to remove my glasses for this trek because they were pretty useless in any kind of precipitation anyway. I refused to consider that it seemed a little easier to see as far as I could—that my eyesight might have improved recently.

That was another thing I didn't want to think about, because it would loop me back to the first thing.

I blinked against the snowflakes catching in my bangs and eyelashes, looking for other signs of life. Although the snow and clouds reflected the streetlights of town, everything seemed so dark and lifeless now compared to a month ago. All the holiday lights and decorations had come down a couple of weeks ago, after the Festival of Lights on January eighth, plunging us into what I called the dark days of winter. Although our town was normally booked solid with festivals and special events, January only had two. The next one wasn't until the end of the month—the Winter Carnival. If it weren't for skiing and snowboarding, the first month of the year would be pure suckage here in Havenwood Falls. Thank Goddess for the slopes.

Not that I would have much time for them this season. I had a few things on my plate. Well, one big thing. I was hoping tonight's meeting of the Court of the Sun and the Moon, the governing body of the supernatural residents in our town—Who was I kidding? They were the true rulers of all the town: supe, human, and anything else that moved. Anyway, I hoped they'd give me permission tonight to focus solely on one particular task—saving a certain Asshole Extraordinaire I couldn't seem to quit and my best friend's parents, all of whom were trapped within the same curse, though in different ways. A curse they trusted me to figure out how to break, supposedly with the Eye of Valerian, an old dark artifact trapped in its protective cage and tucked safely away in a lockbox at home.

"Ah, there you are!" Speak of the devil. As I passed the fountain at the center of the square, my best friend since kindergarten, Michaela Petran, rushed up, falling into step next to me. If I hadn't recognized her voice, I might not have recognized her at all. She was so bundled up in her parka, knit hat, scarf, and gloves, that I could barely see anything of her except her green-gray eyes, the eyes of the moroi vampires. Moroi meant she was mortal, which also meant she was not impervious to the cold, unlike some of the other vampires in town. "What a ridiculous night for a Court meeting."

Michaela had claimed the Petran seat on the Court a few months ago to represent her family and the other local vampires. The seat had been left vacant by her parents and then her aunt, who'd all died in recent years. Their final deaths were all part of said curse I was determined to break.

I was the Court's business manager, a position I'd been given shortly after high school graduation as part of my grooming to take the Beaumont seat sometime in the future, after both my grandmother and my mother died. That could be centuries, though. Thanks to our magic, we lived quite a bit longer than the average human. So yeah, I probably had centuries of this job to look forward to. Having Michaela on the Court now made it a little more bearable. At least now when things happened that nobody else in town could know about, I had someone to talk about it with. Not that I was a gossip or anything. But in our town, crazy shit happened, and on a pretty regular basis. Sometimes a person just needed to talk about it.

"Do you need me to warm you?" I offered, already pulling my hands out of my pockets.

Michaela pushed in closer to me. "You're the best!"

With a few murmured words and a twist of my fingers, we were cocooned in a bubble of warm air. The spell was such a tiny blip of energy, I didn't worry about anyone noticing or caring.

"I was at the bookstore today, and Sedona's ordering me a bunch of bridal magazines," Michaela said, rambling on with excitement. "Of course, I'm not bothering Xandru with it, and you don't have to worry, either. I won't really get serious about planning until this whole thing with Tase and . . . everyone . . . is cleared up, but when we started looking at all the different ones she could order, I got a little . . . enthused. Sorry."

"No worries. I'm glad at least one of us has a distraction." I hadn't missed how she'd stammered over the issue with Tase and her parents, not even bringing them up specifically. Anybody who didn't know Michaela might have thought she dismissed their dire situation because she was more concerned about her wedding than the fact that they were cursed to a special part of Hell called the Infernum. Those of us who did know her would see right through her efforts to pretend like it didn't bother her as much as it really did. Looking at bridal books truly was a necessary distraction for her.

Michaela was a bit of a control freak. It made her good at her job —owning and managing Whisper Falls Inn and organizing all of its special events—as well as taking care of her teenage sister and brother, though she was only twenty-five herself. It did not make her good at waiting and sitting on the sidelines, having to rely on others to solve her problems. I'd rather have her oohing and ahhing over wedding dresses than hounding me every day about my progress. I got enough of that from the Rocas.

After crossing Stuart Street, we turned to go around to the back of City Hall, where there was a lone, quite innocuous-looking metal door with a moon logo embossed into it. My grandmother Saundra and eternal dickhead Roman Bishop had just slipped through the door as we rounded the corner. Michaela and I picked up our pace, knowing if Roman had arrived, the meeting was close to starting. He was usually the last to join the rest of the Court, not to be bothered with waiting on anyone else.

Entering the door and heading down the steps to the basement, we quickly caught up to Saundra and Roman, who strode down the long hallway in silence. Both of them had obviously used a warming charm, because neither was dressed appropriately for the weather. Saundra had exchanged her normal skirt suit for dress pants, but her coat was not nearly thick enough to do much good against the cold. And Roman wore his usual thousand-dollar dress pants (I hated to admit how nicely he filled them out) and a leather coat—again, not heavy enough for tonight's storm. They both wore expensive Italian leather shoes better suited for the Mediterranean coastline than the mountains of Colorado.

They were always jumping down supes' throats for doing stupid things, like riding motorcycles in the winter, not because of the cold or potential danger, but because no normal human would dare such a feat, and it would look suspicious. But here they were, dressed for a party in the tropics during our worst blizzard of the season. Hypocrites. I wondered what the members of SIN, our local motorcycle club, would think about that, but thinking of them led me down a different path of thought I preferred to avoid. So I was grateful when we reached the double wooden doors at the end of the hall that opened up to the Court's meeting space.

The room was large, with a dais on the opposite wall, where there was a table and several chairs lined up behind it. Most of those chairs were already occupied with the other members of the Court. Michaela hurried up to her seat, while Saundra strode with deliberation up the center aisle and Roman sauntered his way in that direction. Below the dais, spread out through most of the rest of the room, were rows of chairs, furnished for a large audience. There rarely ever was one, including tonight. So those chairs were all empty—until I took a seat in the front row. I usually sat at my desk back in the corner and took notes from there, but I knew I'd be put front and center tonight, so I may as well take the position now.

While everyone settled, I produced a notebook and pen in my lap and began jotting down the members in attendance, all of them leaders of their respective Old Families: Lawrence Mills, aka Old Man Mills, frost dragon shifter (he probably delighted in tonight's weather); Elsmed Fairchild, fae of the Seelie Court; Michaela, moroi vampire; Saundra Beaumont, witch and High Priestess of the Luna Coven; Mathilde Augustine, witch and High Priestess of the Luna Coven; Roman Bishop, warlock and High Priest of the Luna Coven; Lilith Blackstone, witch hunter; and Mayor Barbara Stuart, human (the only one on the Court). I also noted that Siobhan McFeeny (Spring Court fae) and Odette Alverson (siren) were absent, and Mayor Barbie said she'd be their proxy for any votes tonight.

Sheriff Ric Kasun, wolf shifter, sat at the end of the table, too. He didn't have voting privileges, but he'd been in this canyon long before any of the Old Families had arrived, and he was head of our local law enforcement. For those reasons, he was present at the meetings and gave input on many matters.

There was no real leader of the Court—they all had equal votes—but Saundra often took the lead of the meetings, as she did tonight. After calling the meeting to order, she tilted her head toward me, her gray hair in its usual twist, her forehead wrinkling above brown eyes very similar to my own.

"Do you have any news on the situation regarding Atanase Roca and Irina and Mihail Petran?" she asked me, her voice formal.

"Not much more to report since last time," I replied, referring to the emergency meeting called after Harper Sinclair had channeled the Petrans from their entrapment in the Infernum for the second time.

Harper, a psychic scribe who was still learning how to use and control her powers, had inadvertently contacted the Petrans on New Year's Day the first time. Their information had led me to find and obtain the Eye of Valerian, which had wreaked havoc in the lives of those I cared about greatly—the Petrans and the Rocas.

"No news about the skinwalker who had been trying to steal the

Eye of Valerian," I added. The creature had taken the shape of a former member of my coven and claimed that she worked for someone called the Collector.

"You mean the shapeshifter," Mathilde clarified, and several heads turned toward her. "Madame Luiza called it a skinwalker, but it is not of the same ilk as those of Native American origins. This one did not behave in the same way, and the skin it left behind did not have the same properties. We've tested it. It's the same creature who'd been at the inn last summer, but it's not a skinwalker. We shouldn't call it that."

"No news about the shapeshifter," I said, correcting myself.

"And the Collector she mentioned?" Old Man Mills asked. "Anything more about him?"

Michaela's eyes caught mine momentarily as my gaze traveled to the old man. After the events of that night, she and I had speculated if Mills himself was the person the shapeshifter had blamed, since dragons liked treasure and he owned the local pawn shop. But we didn't even know if the Collector was real or if the shapeshifter had simply been trying to distract us with a made-up story before it escaped.

"No, nothing," I said. "If anybody knows anything, they're keeping an impossible secret."

"The people in this town are used to keeping impossible secrets," Saundra said pointedly.

"Then we must work harder in discovering who this Collector is," Elsmed said, thumping his fist on the table. "He could be anyone in this town, and a danger to us all."

"Or he could be no one," Roman drawled, his dark blue eyes sliding over each of the other Court members as if in challenge. Michaela and I looked at each other again. "And he's done nothing to threaten anybody yet."

"I'm sorry, but what about the Petran boy?" Mathilde demanded. "And Atanase? All of our vampires could have been destroyed—or do the destroying, affected by that Eye of Valerian the Collector wanted so badly. Look what's happened to all the Petrans and the Rocas already!"

"I assume someone has questioned Atanase about the Collector," Old Man Mills said. "It seems he got himself tied up with this person. He probably has information."

I peered at the old dragon, wondering if he thought we were dumb enough to not start with Tase or if he was trying to throw us off his scent.

"Addie and I have both questioned him," Sheriff Kasun said.

Old Man Mills pulled back. "In Elsmed's presence?"

"Yes, in my presence," Elsmed, a mind reader, said. "Tase thought he was working with Magda the whole time. If he knows anything about the Collector, he has a good way of hiding those thoughts from me."

He and Old Man Mills both turned their frosty gazes on me. It was no secret I carried an amulet that protected my thoughts from Elsmed's intrusion. Many of us who knew about him did.

"If he does, he didn't get it from me," I said, holding up my hands in innocence. "But I'm fairly certain he knows nothing about this Collector person. He's so anxious to break the curse on himself that he's pretty much giving in to my every request. I think he would have told me by now, so I could focus all my energy on the Eye of Valerian. And I'm honestly hoping you will decide tonight that I may do just that."

"I agree with Lawrence, though. This Collector could be a real threat," Mayor Barbie said, running her hand up the back of her fluffy pink bouffant.

Michaela piped up. "Look, all of us who were in the cave with the shapeshifter that night have already told you what we think—that Faux-Magda seemed to throw the idea of the Collector out as a last-ditch effort to take the heat off of herself. Until we have some other kind of proof, we don't even know if the Collector exists. In the meantime, Addie could be wasting her time tracking down a fictional character instead of focusing on the Eye of Valerian and breaking the curse on Tase and . . . my parents."

Knowing her as well as I did, I could hear the very slight tremor in her voice as she said those last two words. She sat back, staring at the far wall, her chest lifting as she inhaled deeply. I knew she was fighting either tears or an angry outburst. The mention of her parents, who had been close friends with nearly everybody on the Court, quieted them for a moment.

"Michaela is right." Roman broke the silence. Michaela and I exchanged another look, this one of surprise. Roman never agreed with her or me. In fact, he seemed to enjoy making our lives as difficult as possible. He was the last person I'd expect to do anything that would lighten my load. "With no further proof of this person's existence, we have little choice but to accept Michaela and Adelaide's theory that the shapeshifter mentioned the Collector as a scapegoat. A falsity to distract us. I, for one, don't believe in wasting my time on lies. Adelaide needs to focus on the Eye of Valerian and breaking the curse to protect our town from Tase." He paused, then seemed to add as an afterthought, "And to free the Petrans, of course."

Then I understood. Roman, along with his brother Ronan and their company Bishop Enterprises, had business dealings with Tase. The curse on Tase might have been a strain on Roman's bottom line. Either that, or Roman was the one doing the distracting—downplaying the truth of the Collector because he himself knew more about him.

Or because he actually *was* the Collector.

That had been another theory Michaela and I had briefly discussed the other day, after Harper had channeled the Petrans a second time—the day we'd learned that the Eye of Valerian was the secret to breaking their curse and I was the one to do it.

By the time the Court meeting concluded, I'd been ordered to focus my time and energy on the dark artifact and breaking the curse, the shapeshifter's story about the Collector dismissed and quickly forgotten.